Have Courage, Be Kind

THE TALE OF

Dɪsɴᴇʏ

CINDERELLA

Have Courage, Be Kind

THE TALE OF

Dᴉsɴᴇʏ

CINDERELLA

By Brittany Candau

Based on the Screenplay by Chris Weitz

Executive Producer Tim Lewis

Produced by Simon Kinberg

Allison Shearmur

David Barron

Directed by Kenneth Branagh

Dᴉsɴᴇʏ PRESS
Los Angeles • New York

Printed in the United States of America
First Hardcover Edition, January 2015
1 3 5 7 9 10 8 6 4 2

V381-8386-5-14346

LOC Number: 2014944948

ISBN 978-1-4847-2361-6

For more Disney Press fun, visit www.disneybooks.com.
For more Cinderella fun, visit www.disney.com/cinderella.

For C.P., my very own fairy godmother
—B.C.

For Courtney, my little sister and princess
—C.G.

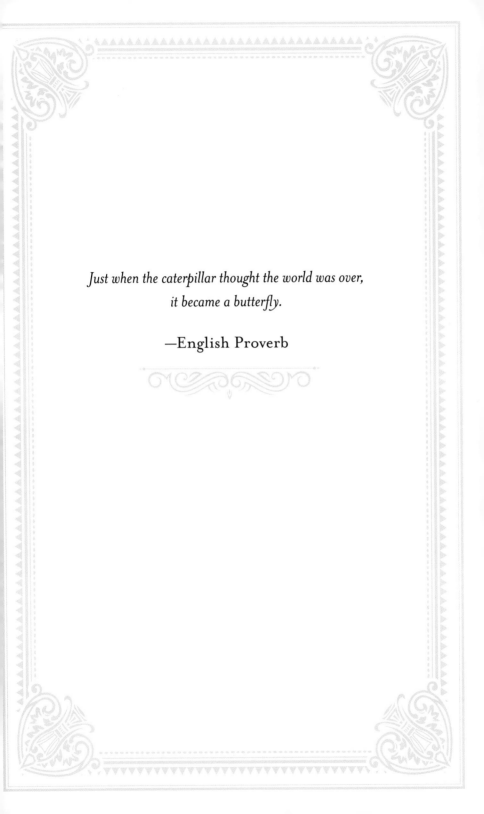

*Just when the caterpillar thought the world was over,
it became a butterfly.*

—English Proverb

ELLA

Chapter 1

THERE were quite a few special things about the five-year-old girl named Ella: the first being that she could already quote Shakespeare, usually her father's favorite lines, but occasionally the particularly funny-sounding ones that made her giggle; the second being that she charmed everyone she met, every man, woman, bird, and beast; and the third being that she, at this very moment, was a mighty elephant.

"HMMMMMM!" the elephant-girl cried, swaying her arm to and fro. She knocked over a few toy blocks and stomped her feet as hard as she could. Then, squinting her eyes, she looked around the hazy savanna for her elephant friends.

Suddenly, a frantic scurrying interrupted the girl's play. "Matilda! Edna!" The glowing sun turned into candlelight. The full trees transformed into long curtains. The waving grass became her soft pink rug. The large watering hole turned into her cozy bed, and the faraway land of Ella's imagination faded into her snug bedroom once more.

She ran to the mice to make sure they were okay, chiding herself for not being more careful. The mice had been roaming in the walls of her room for as long as she could remember. She'd named them after some of her favorite characters in the books her father read to her—Matilda, a charming woman who guided lost souls through a valley, and Edna—a pleasant nurse who could heal anyone. True, neither of these characters were mice exactly, but Ella believed her friends liked the names just the same. They were such lovely companions, so sweet and playful.

However, not everyone saw the mice that way. When the housemaid Helen had found Ella's little whiskered playmates while straightening Ella's room, she had shrieked and rushed downstairs, running into Ella's mother on her way to the kitchen.

"Helen, what's wrong?" Ella's mother had asked when she saw the frantic woman rushing toward her.

"I hate to tell you this, miss," Helen replied. "But Ella's room has been *infested*. There are at least two rodents in there, the dirty creatures. We must get the rat poison straightaway."

"No!" Both Helen and Ella's mother turned to look at Ella who had been quietly trailing behind Helen. Ella's mother bent down so she was at eye-level with her daughter.

"Yes, sweetheart?"

Taking a deep breath, Ella had explained to her mother and to Helen that Matilda and Edna were not dirty creatures at all—they were very polite. She was sure that they would not cause any trouble.

Ella's mother had listened solemnly, understanding in her bright eyes. Ella found that her mother understood most things.

"Quite right. Thank you, darling," she'd said. Then, to Ella's relief, she'd asked Helen to promise not to disturb the mice. And the housemaid had done so, albeit begrudgingly.

Now, after all that, Ella had frightened the poor dears.

"I'm sorry," she called to the small crack in the wall in which the mice had disappeared. "Come back and play!"

Edna came out first, sniffing the air cautiously. At the sight of Ella, she let out a joyful squeak and approached the little girl. Matilda followed close behind, twitching her whiskers in a friendly manner.

"I will be a more careful elephant next time," Ella

promised. Ella sat on the floor, and the mice crawled into her lap, snuggling against the folds of her dress. Ella smiled down at them, using her forefinger to pet the soft fur on Edna and Matilda's heads.

"Perhaps now would be a good time for a bedtime story," Ella suggested. She was quiet for a moment, forming a new tale in her mind. Then she began. "Once upon a time, there lived a very friendly elephant . . ."

Early the next morning, long after Ella had finished her story and put the mice to bed, and long after Ella's mother had put Ella herself to bed, the sound of singing wafted through Ella's open window. It mixed with the sounds of a bleating sheep and chirping sparrows.

"Lavender's blue, dilly dilly . . ."

"Mother!" Ella cried. She sprang out of bed and raced out of her bedroom, across the hall, and down the stairs to the kitchen—her shortcut to the back door. She had not put on her shoes, but she didn't care. Shoes could be such a bother, anyway.

"Whoa, there," the family's cook called after her. "And where are you off to in such a hurry, Miss Ella?"

Ella stopped, her face flushed. "Why, to see Mother outside, Flora! Would you like to come?"

It was a well-known fact that Ella loved nothing more than to be outdoors. She often had to be persuaded to come back *inside*, even when it was pouring rain or as dark as pitch. Whenever anyone from the home went out to tend to the gardening, or to feed the chickens and horses, or simply to enjoy the fresh air, Ella would jump at the opportunity to join them.

"That's all right, dear, I've got breakfast to tend to," Flora said, gesturing to a simmering pot on the stove. "But you take some water to your mother."

Flora grabbed a pitcher from the counter and poured some of its contents into a cup, then handed it off to Ella. After giving Flora a careful curtsy, Ella hurried out the door.

She found her mother next to the shepherd called James, kneeling in front of a ewe. The sheep lay on one side, bleating loudly. The rest of the flock grazed on the grass nearby.

As she heard Ella approach, Ella's mother motioned to her. "Ella, come quick! Peppy is having her lamb!"

Ella ran to her mother's side and gaped at the scene before her. It was miraculous and strange all at once. Trying to decide where she'd be of most use, Ella moved over to Peppy's head, patting her as soothingly as she could. She encouraged the sheep to drink out of the cup meant for her mother.

Ella's mother smiled and nodded approvingly as

she and the shepherd continued their work. "Singing seems to help," she told her daughter.

Without hesitation, Ella broke into her favorite song, the lullaby she sang with her mother every night.

"Lavender's blue, dilly dilly . . ."

"Lavender's green," her mother continued.

"When I am king, dilly dilly, you shall be queen . . ." they sang together.

"There!" Ella's mother cried.

Peppy shifted, and at that moment, Peppy's lamb greeted the world. The sheep turned to clean her baby as Ella's mother and the shepherd cheered.

"Here he is!" James exclaimed.

"Well done, my love," Ella's mother said, pulling her daughter into a tight hug.

Ella watched the little lamb nuzzle against his mother. "He's so sweet," she observed. Then inspiration struck her. "Benedick. We should call him Benedick."

"Names have power, you know . . . magic." James looked at Ella with a twinkle in his eye. "And that is a big name for such a wee lamb."

Ella considered this. "Yes. But he will grow," she answered matter-of-factly.

"Indeed he will," James agreed. "Indeed he will."

Just like Benedick, Ella grew, as little lambs and little girls tend to do. Five years passed, and though Ella was now taller, knew her letters and numbers (in multiple languages, at that), and had started to wear shoes more often, her vast imagination and her immense capacity to love did not change.

Ella's mother often said it took a village to keep a home, so Ella made a point of aiding the workers of the household, folding a clean sheet here, adding salt to a soup there, spreading fresh hay in the stables.

It should be said that all of the members of the staff brightened when they saw Ella's shining face. They often observed that by some remarkable instinct, this little girl could sense what others needed at any given time—a funny story, a listening ear, a helping hand. Whatever was needed, Ella tried her best to provide.

And whenever Ella received the nods and smiles and embraces of appreciation for her efforts, it warmed her heart. She truly believed there was nothing better than helping someone or brightening a person's day. And she knew that every member of the household would do the same for her if she ever needed help or a good cheering up.

Ella also spent her days going on adventures with her very best friend, her mother. They would take long strolls in the countryside, tend to the plants in the greenhouse, and ride horses through the pastures. For Ella, there was nothing better than galloping in an open field, the cool wind at her back, her mother at her side.

Ella's father was a merchant, and as such, was often away on business. But whenever he was home, oh, was it a celebration. He would take her into his study and they would spend hours reading their favorite books aloud. He would teach her the languages he'd learned on his trips, and show her the world on massive, brightly-colored maps.

Then, in the evenings, Ella and her mother and father would dance and play and eat hearty feasts prepared by Mother and Flora using all the ripe vegetables from the garden. The house was never so full of life and music as when the three of them were together.

One particular afternoon, Ella was feeding the birds in the back meadow and missing her father terribly. He'd been gone for almost a month, and was due back anytime. She and her mother had decided that they would make his favorite dessert, pumpkin pudding, when he returned.

"You there! What d'you think you're doing?" Ella cried out. She had been so distracted thinking of her father that she hadn't noticed the throng of ducks, goats, and sheep trying to get at the bread crumbs before the smaller sparrows and finches had a chance.

"Let the little ones have their share," she scolded, moving the larger animals out of the way. She picked up one particular goat who was chomping furiously.

"Goliath—*do* take time to chew your food. We don't want you getting an upset stomach."

"Do you still believe that they understand you?"

Ella turned to see her mother watching over them, her lips formed into a soft smile. Ella put Goliath down.

"Don't they, Mother?"

Her mother took a step closer, putting a gentle hand on Ella's shoulder.

"Oh, yes. I believe that animals listen and speak to us, if only we have the ear for it. That is how we learn to look after them."

Ella watched the birds and goats eating their snack, giving one another space to move now. It did seem as though they had listened to her. And Matilda and Edna had remained the captive audience of her stories. But if they looked after the animals . . .

"Who looks after us?" Ella asked.

"Fairy godmothers, of course," her mother answered without skipping a beat. She took Ella's arm in hers as they walked around the meadow.

"And you believe in them?"

"I believe in everything."

Ella considered this. "Then I believe in everything, too."

"Which is just as it should be," Ella's mother said, smiling broadly.

Ella returned her smile and then looked down. "Oh!" she let out a little gasp.

Kneeling in the grass to get a closer look, she carefully scooped up what looked like a trembling ball of fuzz. It was a scrawny baby bird, clearly too small to be away from its nest. She held it toward her mother, who had knelt next to her.

"Where is its home?" Ella whispered, not wanting to disturb the little thrush.

Ella's mother put a finger to her lips and tilted her head. Ella couldn't help thinking that her mother looked so beautiful in that moment, the wind blowing dandelion fuzz through her hair. She looked just like the forest fairies of storybooks.

Suddenly, Ella's mother rose and walked to a nearby hedge. She peered through the brambles and then very gently parted the leaves. Lo and behold, on a twisted bramble sat a nest with four other baby thrushes. The little birds were straining their necks and squawking.

Ella slowly handed the thrush in her small hands to her mother, who gently placed it with its brothers and sisters.

"Now watch," Ella's mother whispered.

Sure enough, at that moment, a red-chested bird flew through the air, little worms dangling from its

mouth. Landing on the nest, she began to feed all five babies. Then she looked round to Ella and her mother. The mama bird sweetly bobbed her head at them.

It seemed Ella's mother had been right! Humans and animals really could understand one another.

Ella's mother put her arms around her daughter's shoulders. "She wants to thank you," she whispered.

"She doesn't have to," Ella said shyly.

But Ella didn't get a chance to continue the conversation with the thrush. For at that very moment, they were interrupted by the sound of hoofbeats. Someone was coming!

Ella felt a rush of excitement. She couldn't believe it. That had to be her father! Her father was finally home! She and her mother exchanged grins.

"Run along, then," her mother prompted.

After kissing her mother's cheek, Ella rushed down the slope of the meadow toward the forest path her father took to get home.

She rounded the curve of the treelined trail, spotting her father and his traveling companion, Farmer John, on the horse-drawn cart.

She waved as she sprinted toward them. "Papa! Papa!"

As soon as he saw her, Ella's father slowed his faithful horse, Galahad, to a stop and hopped down from the cart. Then he scooped Ella up into his arms and twirled her around.

"Welcome home, Papa!" Ella cried.

"Ella!" her father exclaimed, tilting her down so she could pet Galahad's muzzle and greet Farmer John before leading them to the stone fountain in front of the house.

After setting Ella on the fountain's edge, Father reached into his coat pocket and produced a small green parcel.

"What is it?" Ella asked.

"Oh, nothing but a cocoon. I found it hanging on a tree," he replied. Ella scrunched her nose, knowing her father was teasing her. He winked before continuing. "But I *think* there may be something inside."

Ella grinned. Then she carefully opened the ornate wrapping. Inside she found a pretty toy butterfly on a golden handle.

It was extraordinary—a creature composed of soft lavenders and blush pinks. Ella marveled at the gift. It was so delicate it looked as though it might fall apart by a mere touch.

Ella's father grabbed the gleaming handle and jiggled the butterfly around Ella's head. It flapped and fluttered easily, clearly much sturdier and more capable than it looked.

Ella clapped her hands in delight.

"In French, that is *un papillon*," he explained, continuing the French lesson they'd started before he'd left.

"*Un papillon*," Ella repeated, her eyes still trained on the toy butterfly.

At that moment, Ella's mother appeared at the front of the house, a smile on her face as she watched her two very favorite people in the world. She always insisted that Ella and her father greet one another first whenever he returned from his journeys, explaining that she wanted them to have a proper hello before she stepped in.

"*Très bon*," Ella's father was saying, praising his daughter's French. Setting the toy butterfly on the fountain, he nimbly hopped to his feet and offered his hand. "*Voulez-vous danser, mademoiselle?*"

Ella giggled. "*S'il vous plaît!*"

Placing her small feet upon her father's large, booted ones, the pair waltzed up to Ella's mother. Ella's mother started to sing, producing a sweet tune for their dance.

"Merry along, merry away,
ev'ry dawn and ev'ry day . . ."

When they got closer to the house, Ella and her father opened their formation, gesturing for Ella's mother to join them. Ella's mother beamed.

The three of them danced and sang, laughing as they circled round and round, hands clasped.

From afar, they looked like a trio of bright moving colors against the blue sky and beige stone walls, a watercolor painting of happiness itself.

Chapter 2

THE room swam in and out of focus as Ella tried to fight off sleep. She was so happy her family was reunited once more. And even after an evening of listening to Father's stories, of eating the delicious pumpkin pudding, and of playing little games and reading big books, all she wanted to do was spend more time with her parents.

But, alas, Ella found herself in that twilight place between slumber and wakefulness as her mother sang her trusty lullaby.

> *"Lavender's blue, dilly dilly,*
> *Lavender's green . . ."*

She felt her mother gently smooth the blankets over her. Her father stood behind her, casting his loving gaze.

On her bedside table, all the various treasures Father had brought Ella over the years glistened and gleamed—a pretty doll from Paris, a porcelain bowl from China, a vibrant feather quill from Spain. The toy butterfly had proudly been placed in front of them all, a place of honor.

Ella shifted in her bed, forcing herself to keep her eyes open for as long as possible. She joined her mother in singing the last verse.

> *"Lavender's green, dilly dilly,*
> *Lavender's blue . . .*
> *You must love me*
> *for I love you . . ."*

She looked at her parents standing close to one another and smiling down at her. Then Ella squinted, noticing something she hadn't seen before. They both looked tired, dark circles under the eyes, as though they were worn out. Of course, Father had had a long journey. And Mother hadn't sat down all day.

They need to sleep, Ella realized. *There will be tomorrow.*

Now content to drift off to sleep, Ella leaned over to her night table and blew out the small Moroccan lantern illuminating the room, another one of her father's gifts from his travels.

"Go to bed, Mother, go to bed, Father," Ella

proclaimed as she snuggled back into her bed. "It is time you had some rest."

Ella's parents looked at one another, both appreciating how aware, how observant their profound little girl seemed to be. Tomorrow would be another day.

The next day was indeed another day, and the family had a score of tomorrows. One such day, Ella sat with her father in his study. He was supposed to be doing something with his accounts—*reconciling*, Ella remembered him calling it. But that was far too boring. He'd announced that he much preferred spending time with his daughter. So instead, he and Ella were playing their favorite game.

" 'There is no book so bad . . . that it does not have something good in it,' " Ella prompted.

Her father thought for a bit, leaning back in his comfy armchair. "Hmmm . . . that would be *Don Quixote*. Now I have a tough one for you. Prepare yourself."

Ella perched on her knees in her own chair and leaned forward. "Yes?" she giggled, failing to match her father's comically stoic expression.

" 'We know no time when we were not as now,' " her father said, lifting his finger dramatically.

"Paradise Lost," Ella answered.

"Oh, I was sure I had you! When did my beautiful daughter become so wise?"

" 'Beauty without intelligence is like a hook without bait,' " Ella said without skipping a beat.

"Ho! *Tartuffe!* I am beaten," Ella's father laughed, throwing his hands up. "Well done, miss. Well done."

Ella leaned back in her chair, quite content. For a few moments, she and her father sat in companionable silence, him looking at the stack of papers on his desk, her gazing at the mountainous bookshelves displaying well-worn spines.

"Father, where will you be going on your next journey?" Ella asked. As much as she hated to see him go, she was fond of hearing about his adventures to other lands.

"Oh, well, my dear, I don't have another trip planned for a while."

Ella looked at him questioningly. Her father always had a trip planned. Such was the life of a merchant.

"Your mother hasn't been feeling well," he explained, his kind eyes crinkling with worry. Then, seeing her look of concern, he hurried to continue. "It's nothing serious, of course. She thinks it's just a bit of hay fever. But I thought I'd better stay until she's feeling more herself."

Ella nodded and smiled at her father reassuringly.

They resumed their game. But Ella couldn't stop picturing the flash of distress on her father's face, nor could she quiet the voice in her head that reminded her that something was not quite right.

Her mother had always been the picture of health. It was not like her to be sick, or to even speak up if she was feeling poorly. Normally, Ella or one of the household staff had to notice a chorus of sneezes before telling Ella's mother to go to bed and drink some honey tea. Ella sighed under the guise of trying to figure out where her father's next quote came from. Everything would be all right. It had to be.

"All's Well That Ends Well," she proclaimed, answering her father's clue.

It started out like any other summer day. Ella had risen to the rooster's cry. She'd given bread crumbs to Matilda and Edna, now a bit older and slower, but friendly as ever. She'd greeted Helen, who was dusting in the parlor, and Flora, who was on her way to the market. Then she'd peered in on her sleeping mother, who was spending her days resting in Father's study as of late.

Ella narrowed her eyes in concern. The doctor was coming back today. Certainly, he would help heal her mother. He would bring the latest remedies that would transform her mother back into her strong, vibrant self.

Quietly, Ella headed down the hall and outside to greet the animals. She dispersed the feed on the grass as birds and beasts alike rushed over to eat their breakfast. Peering down, she tried to make sure that everyone got a fair share.

Ella thought of all the times she'd done this very thing with her mother. Before she could stop them, tears of worry sprang to her eyes. Trying to take a deep breath, she felt the air catch in her throat. She slowly backed up against the fountain and lowered herself onto the ledge. The sparrows chirped at her feet while the ducks quacked worriedly.

"It's all right," she told them. "We have to be strong. For Mother, remember?"

Just then, Ella realized what would clear her head. Riding. She never felt better than when she was astride a horse, galloping through the open fields or the shady forest. She quickly finished her morning chores and headed to the stable.

"What do you say, old boy? You up for a ride?" Ella asked Galahad, patting his nose.

Galahad whinnied in agreement. Though he was her father's horse, Galahad and Ella had always had a special connection. And today, he was the one she wanted to share her adventure with.

Soon Ella and Galahad were racing up and down the neighboring hills, the wind in her hair and in his mane. Ella felt as though she were flying. She was finally able to take deep breaths of the fresh air, comforted by Galahad's quick and steady gallop.

Finally, Ella slowed Galahad to a stop at the top of a hill. From up here, her home looked lovely as ever, with its stately stones, its large fountain, and its greenhouse sparkling in the sunlight. The windows winked and the warm wooden doors seemed to say, "Please, come in!" It was such a lovely place. She could see why her parents were so proud of it, why they took such pains to keep it up.

"Time to go home, old boy," she told Galahad, feeling better. "Let's get you a treat."

It was only back in the stables, as she was giving the horses sugar cubes and more hay, that she realized how still everything was. How quiet. Something did not feel right. She wondered how much time had passed, wondered where everyone was.

Suddenly, she heard Flora's frantic voice from the stable door.

"Ella, come quick," she said. "Your father is calling for you."

Ella looked at Flora's face, saw the tears brimming in her eyes. Her heart dropped like a stone. Closing Galahad's stable door, Ella hurried with Flora back into the house, past other solemn members of the household. The study door was closed. Ella sank into a chair just outside, waiting.

Finally, the door swung open to a grave picture. The doctor was putting tools away in his bag. Her mother was on the duvet, her pale face grimacing. Her father hovered nearby. He shared a meaningful look with the doctor before seeing him out.

Noticing Ella in the hall, her father put his arm around her. "Ella. Come," he said, his voice wavering.

Ella cast an uneasy glance his way and then headed to her mother's side, reaching out to hold a pale hand. She noticed her mother's wedding ring, a gold band holding a flower made out of pearls and a single ruby. Its simple elegance had always suited her mother. Now it seemed as though it was going to slip off her frail finger.

"Mother?"

Her mother turned her head and smiled. Then she started to speak, her voice soft but clear. "Ella, it seems it is time for me to leave. And we must say good-bye before I go."

Ella felt a prickle of tears behind her eyes. No. It was too soon. She could not say good-bye to her mother. Her beautiful mother who was always so full of life and song. Who had so much more to teach her.

"I don't want you to be sad," Ella's mother continued. Then, noticing the tears falling down her daughter's face, she shook her head wistfully. "Well, you can be sad for a little while. But then, whenever you think of me, I want you to smile. Because I'll be smiling too, when I look at you."

Ella tried to make herself respond, to reassure her mother that she'd be okay. But her throat was tight. All she could do was nod.

Ella's mother attempted to sit up, but couldn't get her head off the pillow. Ella leaned in closer, smoothing the blankets as her mother had done so many times for her.

"I want to tell you a secret," her mother said. "A great secret that will see you through all the trials that life has to offer."

Ella leaned even closer, trying to take in every bit of this moment. Her mother continued. "You must always remember this: *Have courage, and be kind.* You have more kindness in your little finger than most people possess in their whole body. And it has power. More than you know."

"Kindness has power?" Ella asked, wiping the hot tears off her cheek.

"And magic," Ella's mother responded. "Truly.

Where there is kindness, there is goodness. And where there is goodness, there is happiness. Have courage, and be kind. Will you promise me?"

"I promise," Ella said.

Her mother sighed, looking relieved at delivering this last message. Then she smiled woefully. "Good . . . good. Now I have to go, my love. Forgive me."

The words struck Ella painfully as she realized this was it. This was the last day she would spend with her mother. The last time she would hear her mother's voice. The last time she would hold her mother's hand. She searched deep inside, looking for the words that would help her mother in this moment, the kindest words she knew in this new sad world.

"Of course I forgive you," Ella said, wrapping her arms around her mother. Behind them, Ella's father joined the hug, silently sobbing as he held his two girls. The trio held one another that way for a while, holding onto their last precious moments together.

Chapter 3

THE years passed. Summers rolled into falls, falls to winters, winters to springs. Every year, on her mother's birthday, Ella and her father would gather daisies from the meadow—her mother's favorite flower. Then Ella would put them in little vases and jars all over the house. It brightened things for a time, returned some of the light that had gone after her mother had passed.

Otherwise, Ella kept herself busy tending to her father, the house, and its members, as well as the animals and garden, believing that in order to uphold her promise to her mother, she must not wallow in her grief. She must do everything possible to continue the life she'd started with the wonderful woman who'd raised her. And above all, she must continue to have courage and be kind, even to herself, even when it was difficult.

To her surprise, things did get easier. The pain lessened. And while the memory of her mother never grew fainter, the heartache did.

While all this occurred, Ella grew into a beautiful young woman; the very picture of her mother, in fact, with blonde, curly hair and warm brown eyes.

"Oh!" Flora started one day, while they were harvesting honey together. "The way you inspected that comb. That is . . . *was* . . . so much like her."

Ella smiled gratefully. She put a gloved hand on Flora's. "Thank you," she said.

Unlike her father, Ella enjoyed talking about her mother. It helped keep her memory alive. Her father, however, could still not say his wife's name without getting upset. He often had to excuse himself and leave the room whenever she was mentioned.

Ella sighed. There was no good in fretting about her father here. Not while navigating through hives of buzzing bees. She shook off her worries for the time being and turned back to the task at hand.

"We've got a good amount here," Ella announced, holding up a jar filled to the brim with the golden liquid. "Father will be so pleased."

"More importantly, *I'm* pleased." Flora winked. "Think of all the delicious desserts I can make with this lot."

"Yes," Ella laughed. "We can serve them tonight. As part of our bon voyage celebration!"

Ella's father was leaving in the morning for a new journey, and Ella wanted to send him off properly. Her father really hadn't done much traveling in the years since her mother had died. Of course, he'd gone on short trips here and there to fulfill his merchant duties, but he hadn't wanted to leave his study, let alone the home, ever since his wife had passed on.

This was the first big trip he'd seemed even remotely interested in taking for some time. And Ella wanted to encourage him as much as she could. Anything to see that old sparkle back in his eyes, even if it meant not seeing him for a few weeks.

"Come, Flora," Ella announced, gathering up their materials. "Let's go make that feast."

After several more feasts and several more voyages, Ella's father almost seemed to be back to his old self. He now had to use a cane to get by, but his kind, easy smile had returned. He could also talk about Ella's mother now, telling and retelling stories about their love until both he and Ella had tears shining in their eyes.

He traveled to more and more exotic and foreign lands, telling Ella about the wonders he'd seen. They practiced their French, Spanish, and Italian together, and read all the books their ever-expanding library contained.

One golden afternoon, Ella sat reading aloud in the drawing room, her father happily munching on a piece of honeyed toast across from her. Though many years had passed, the home was still as warm and comforting as ever, a place of joy and peace.

" 'And thence home, my wife and I singing to our great content, and if ever there were a man happier in his fortunes, I know him not.' " Ella put the book down on the end table and helped herself to a piece of toast. "Thus ends Mr. Pepys. I do love a happy ending, don't you?"

"They are quite my favorite sort," her father agreed.

"As well they should be." Ella grinned.

Ella's father returned her smile; he often said that her smile was so radiant, it was literally impossible not to smile back at her. But then, quite suddenly, his features formed a frown. When he began to speak next, he did so with an air of hesitation. "Ella . . . I have come to the conclusion . . . that perhaps I may begin a new chapter."

"Indeed, Father? I'm glad to hear it," Ella said,

putting her toast down. This was a good sign. Perhaps her father was planning on taking up a hobby or looking into a new trade. That would be so good for him.

Her father continued. "You will recall that some time ago in my travels I made the acquaintance of Sir Francis Tremaine."

"Yes." Ella searched her mind to recall the name. "The master of the Mercer's Guild, is he not?"

"*Was,*" her father corrected. "The poor man has died, alas."

Ella frowned. "I am grieved to hear it, Father."

There was a slight pause. Ella's father cleared his throat. "His widow, an honorable woman, finds herself alone, though still in the prime of her life."

Ella blinked, a wave of clarity hitting her. Her father was seeking the companionship of another, a new wife. But first, he was seeking her approval. A thousand thoughts raced in her mind as a thousand emotions beat against her heart. It all had to do with one simple word. *Mother.*

But Ella knew she could not deprive her father of a new marriage, despite the sinking feeling in her stomach. This was her father's chance at joy again, of relishing life once more. This is what she'd wanted him to do, what her mother would have wanted for him. *Be kind . . .*

After a few moments, Ella gave her father an encouraging smile. "You're worried about telling me. But you mustn't—not if it will lead to your happiness."

"Happiness . . ." her father echoed softly. "Do you think I may have another chance, even though I thought such things were done with?"

"I do, Father."

Her father looked up, touched by his daughter's understanding. He suddenly seemed reenergized. "She would merely be your stepmother. And you would have two lovely sisters to keep you company! So I will know, as far away as I may be, that you are safe at home, cherished and protected."

Not knowing how to respond to this, Ella walked over to her father, putting her arms around him. He hugged her tightly and she pushed her worries aside. She would have to reflect on this change later. For now, all that mattered was that her father was happy. And who knew? This could end up being a wonderful new adventure.

"Does this look all right?" Ella asked Jacqueline and Gus. These mice were just as sociable as their predecessors, Matilda and Edna, had been, and Ella found them to be excellent listeners when she really needed somebody to talk to—particularly somebody who would let her rattle off when she needed to work something out.

She twirled in front of the mice in her favorite blue dress. The mice stared up at her, and Ella flopped down on her bed.

"Oh, you're right. It really doesn't matter what I wear. I just wonder what they'll be like, the Tremaines . . . Perhaps Lady Tremaine will like to garden. And I can show her the greenhouse. And maybe her daughters would like to share my room. We could have great fun, sneaking up food, talking until the wee hours of the night . . ."

She looked down at Jacqueline and Gus. "Of course, they'll have to like mice," she said, smiling. Jacqueline moved her head in what almost looked like a nod of agreement. Gus blinked up at her. Ella burst into laughter. Honestly, it was almost as if those mice could *actually* understand her.

Suddenly, Ella heard the sound of horses and a carriage coming down the drive. A wave of anxiety hit her. Gently patting her friends' little heads, and glancing at the toy butterfly on her night table for luck, Ella raced down the stairs.

"Have courage, be kind," she muttered to herself, squeezing her hands as she joined her father outside.

He smiled at her, a look of cautious hope on his face.

For what seemed like hours, the hired carriage made its way up the drive and stopped in front of them. Two coachmen jumped down, opening the carriage door for their charges.

Ella saw her stepsisters first, one wearing a floral dress in shocking pink, the other in a dress of burnt yellow. They looked around, pointing at one of the footmen to collect their luggage.

"Ah! Anastasia and Drisella," Ella's father called to them. "Meet my daughter, Ella."

"How do you do," Ella said. "I hope you will all be happy here."

At that moment, the group was interrupted by the appearance of another—a beautiful, elegant woman who was dressed in the latest style. A large emerald hat shaded half of her face. She looked so composed as she exited the carriage; no one would guess she'd been traveling for hours. This had to be Lady Tremaine.

As her new stepmother stepped down, Ella noticed she was holding a pink leash attached to a charcoal gray Persian cat. He pranced behind his mistress, and the two, cat and lady, took slow, deliberate glances at their surroundings.

Ella only noticed the woman falter ever so slightly when one of the coachmen approached her. He hovered by her side, obviously waiting for a tip. Lady Tremaine

looked down at her pocketbook, then up again, her face reddening slightly.

Recognizing the situation straightaway, Ella's father stepped forward, handing the coachman a few coins for his trouble. The woman shot a grateful glance at Ella's father.

Ella took a step closer to the pair, getting ready to introduce herself to her new stepmother. But at that moment, Lady Tremaine walked past her and toward the door. Ella's father hurried to follow her.

Feeling that someone, or more accurately, a couple of *someones* were casting intense gazes upon her, Ella turned her attention back to her new stepsisters.

"You have such pretty hair," Anastasia told Ella.

"Thank you," Ella said, touching her golden locks.

"You should have it styled," Drisella added.

Ella paused, not sure what to make of these two. She decided to start again and try to make them feel more at home. "Would you like a tour of the house?" she offered.

"What did she say?" Drisella asked her sister. "Her accent is so twangy."

Anastasia snickered. "She wants to show us her farmhouse. She's proud of it, I think."

"Do they keep animals inside?" Drisella asked.

Ella could not tell if she was joking or not. "Oh, no—" she started to say.

"Dears!" Lady Tremaine suddenly appeared in the doorway, seeming even more serious and majestic than when Ella had first seen her. At first, Ella didn't even notice that her father was standing uncomfortably by her side. "I do hope you won't fuss."

Her declaration made, the coiffed woman turned and headed into the house, and Ella's father trailed behind her.

"After you, Drisella, Anastasia," Ella said, gesturing for the girls to move past her. The two girls giggled and then shuffled toward the door. Ella was not sure if they were amused by her accent again or if she had missed some sort of joke.

Furrowing her brow, Ella moved inside behind them. Upon first glance, the Tremaines were not what she'd expected.

But they have had such a long trip. And they've lost poor Lord Tremaine, she thought, chiding herself. She must be more patient.

Ella joined the others in the drawing room, overhearing her new stepmother talking to her father.

"You did not say that your daughter was so beautiful."

Ella's father beamed proudly. "She takes after her . . ." He stopped short, clearly afraid of offending his new wife.

"Her mother," Lady Tremaine filled in for him. "Just so."

Ella's father smiled at her gratefully.

Meanwhile, Anastasia and Drisella wandered about the room, inspecting everything with their white gloves. Anastasia stopped in front of a large oval mirror, peering at her reflection.

"How long has your family lived here?" Drisella asked.

"Over two hundred years." Ella's father exchanged a happy glance with Ella, who nodded at him encouragingly.

"And in all that time, they never thought to decorate?"

Anastasia snorted at her sister's remark from her post by the mirror.

"Hush, Drisella." Lady Tremaine laughed. "They will think you serious."

At that moment, Ella heard a hissing sound. As the others made their way to the next room, Lady Tremaine leading the way as Ella's father pointed out family heirlooms and Anastasia and Drisella tittered behind, Ella decided to stay back to inspect the noise.

She bent down, finding the Tremaines' gray cat under a table. He was crouched low, teeth bared. Poor little Jacqueline and Gus were shaking in the corner opposite him.

"Oh, no, you don't." Ella intercepted, scooping the gray cat in her arms. Clearly not used to being reprimanded, the cat hissed up at her. She shook her head in reply. "We won't stand any of *that* in this house."

She set the wriggling cat down by the door, and he bolted out of the room, presumably to find his mistress. Jacqueline and Gus scampered in the other direction, clearly not wishing to have another run-in with the new feline member of the home.

"We must all get along," Ella said firmly to the empty room. "We shall have courage and be kind. No matter how difficult."

Chapter 4

I would be safe to say that the next few months proved to be challenging. The Tremaines had grown accustomed to a certain lifestyle, one they found lacking at their new home.

This was all too apparent in the way they displayed their garish works of art, their loud throw pillows, and their satin ribbons tied to everything, including the chandeliers. Their trinkets were arranged in front of the miniature portrait of Ella's mother (no matter how many times Ella slightly shifted them so her mother's face could be seen).

Lady Tremaine also insisted on holding a dinner party every few weeks in order "to uphold their social obligations." These were always elaborate affairs, with the guest list reaching upward of fifty people. A plethora of sparkling wines and extravagant five-course dinners were also deemed necessary, and Ella often found herself in the kitchen helping Flora prepare these lavish meals.

Much to Ella's dismay, her father needed to leave on more and more journeys to keep up with the increasing expenses. For as much as she tried to be amiable with Lady Tremaine and her daughters, even Ella couldn't deny they were difficult. She longed for the company of her dear father, and found herself wishing that things would go back to the way they were before the Tremaines had arrived, despite herself.

One evening, during one of Lady Tremaine's parties, Ella strolled through the candlelit dining room, her hands clasped behind her back. She heard snippets of conversations here and there, mostly about the latest fashions or the current gossip from the village. She hoped she'd find a table discussing literature or travel, something that would pique her interest. She stopped in front of a table where her stepmother, a baron and baroness, and several other notable guests were seated.

"You *are* awful, Baron," Lady Tremaine cackled. "Have you been much at court lately? What is the news of the king?"

"In point of fact," the baron leaned in conspiratorially. "I have heard it from the royal physician that he is not long for the world."

One of the women gasped, putting a gloved hand to her mouth.

"And the prince so young and callow. They say he has no stomach for fighting," Ella's stepmother said.

"Oh, I hear he his quite brave, madam," another guest chimed in. "But he is a dreamy fellow all the same, believes in the rights of man and universal peace. All that sort of nonsense."

The baron harrumphed at that. "Still, if the king commands it, he must go to war again. And that's an end on it."

"How terrible," Ella interjected.

All eyes turned to look upon her. Lady Tremaine narrowed her sharp green ones at her stepdaughter, her discontent at the interruption quite clear.

"Nonsense, my dear," the baron said, responding to her cry. "How else should he prove his mettle?"

Despite Lady Tremaine's glare, Ella did not skip a beat. Wasn't it obvious? "By helping his fellow man, not killing him. No one should be forced to go to war. Neither a prince nor any other poor young fellow."

"Oh, it's quite good for the kingdom," the baron's tablemate argued. "War brings people together and whatnot." He reached up and patted Ella's hand. "But you would not understand. Ladies are such gentle creatures."

Ella was about to reply when Lady Tremaine rose

from her place at the table, glaring down at her. "Ella, can you see that the punch is full?"

Ella looked at her stepmother and the guests. "Certainly," she said agreeably, giving a polite nod before walking past the servants holding trays toward the beverage table.

It was a pity—being called away just when she'd felt she had something to contribute to the conversation. She and her father had often discussed the philosophies of war, the merits of peace. They had studied the great thinkers, such as Plato and Aristotle, and had talked at length about their viewpoints on the subject.

One particular Platonic quote came to mind: "The best is neither war nor faction—they are things we should pray to be spared from—but peace and mutual good will." She made a mental note to try that one on her father the next time they played their game of quotations.

Ella's musings were suddenly interrupted by a familiar growl. "Speaking of war," she said to herself, spotting Lucifer the cat underneath the beverage table. He was in the midst of sneaking up on an unsuspecting Jacqueline, who was nibbling at a bit of cheese that had fallen to the floor.

"Just what do you think you're up to, Lucifer?" Ella asked, picking up the disgruntled kitty. "Jacqueline is my guest. And the eating of guests is not allowed."

At the sound of Ella's voice, Jacqueline looked up and saw her predator. She squeaked gratefully.

"Think nothing of it," Ella told her. "We ladies must help one another."

Lucifer writhed uncomfortably in Ella's arms. "You've got plenty of meat and milk outside to keep you happy," she said, carrying the cat to another room and gently setting him down. "Go on now."

Lucifer let out a disgruntled meow. He was the only animal in the land immune to Ella's kindness.

Ella found her father holed up in his study, poring over papers and making notes with his feather quill.

"You're missing the party," she said, taking a seat in the comfy chair in front of his desk.

Her father looked up. "I imagine it is much like all the other ones." He grinned playfully. Then his smile faltered. "And I'm leaving first thing."

Ella tried to suppress her disappointment at this reminder. But, oh, how she did not want him to leave again! "You're hardly back from the last trip. Do you have to go?"

"I'm afraid so. With . . . a larger household, more bills." Her father waved his hand, gesturing toward the sounds of the uproarious laughter and clinking glasses that had slinked into the room. "I must provide for you all, even if it means a little travel."

"I do not need much," Ella said.

"Not you, no." They looked at one another, knowing they were both thinking about their new family members. Though it would not do to say so. There was nothing they could do about their situation, and as such, there was no use lamenting or regretting what was.

Ella quickly changed the subject. "I have packed your quinine against scurvy, and your Warburg's Physic for the seasickness."

"Capital," her father said gratefully. Then he clapped his hands. "And what would you like me to bring you home from abroad? Your sisters . . . that is, your *stepsisters*," he corrected himself, "have asked for parasols and lace. What will you have?"

"Nothing," Ella replied.

Her father grinned once more. " 'Nothing will come of nothing.' "

"*King Lear*," Ella answered his prompt, laughing.

"Very good!"

Ella thought for a moment. Then she had a burst of inspiration. "I know. Bring me the first branch your shoulder brushes on your journey."

Her father cocked his head. "That is a curious request."

"You'll have to take it with you on your way, and think of me when you look at it," Ella explained, her voice suddenly wavering. She tried to fight off the tears that had started to threaten her composure. For some reason, seeing her father off on this trip was much harder than it had ever been.

"And when you bring it back, it means that you will be with it. And that's what I really want. For you to come back. No matter what."

Ella's father rose, walking around the desk to hug his sweet daughter tightly. "I will," he promised.

He leaned back, studying his daughter's tear-stricken face, and wiped her tears. "Now, Ella," he started gently. "While I'm away, you must be good to your stepmother and stepsisters. Even though they may be . . . *trying* at times."

Ella smiled and nodded, catching his meaning. "I promise."

"Thank you. I always leave a part of me behind, Ella. Remember that. And your mother is here, too, though you see her not. She is the very heart of this place." He looked around as though he could see her kind face on the walls and windows. "That is why we must cherish this house. For her."

Ella nodded once more. She'd often felt the same way. Her memories of her mother were part of the home as much as the sun was part of the sky.

"I miss her," Ella admitted, looking down. "Do you?"

They rarely spoke so openly about Ella's mother these days. It was nice to do so now.

Her father met her eyes, looking aged and wistful. "Very much," he confessed.

As they hugged each other, they did not hear the creak of the floor outside of the study, nor did they suspect that a certain someone had been eavesdropping on their conversation, and had been stung to the core by what she'd overheard.

Chapter 5

THE next morning, Ella's father and Farmer John packed the carriage and readied the horses.

Ella, Lady Tremaine, Anastasia, and Drisella stood at the front of the house to see them off.

"Remember the lace!" Anastasia said. "I simply *must* have it."

"And my parasol!" Drisella added. "For my complexion. That means skin if you don't know."

The men climbed into the cart and the horses started off. The Tremaines headed back inside, but Ella held her father's hand, running with the carriage until the horses sped up to a trot.

"I love you!" she called.

Her father turned around so he could keep his eyes on hers for as long as possible. "I love you!" They waved at one another until the carriage had passed the bend and was out of sight.

Ella scolded herself as she felt the familiar wave of tears brim in her eyes. *That will not do. Crying won't help things.*

She hurried through the door that had been left open by her stepmother and stepsisters, and hastily brushed away the tears.

"Ella, dear." Lady Tremaine's voice rang through the foyer. Ella turned toward the sound and entered the drawing room.

Her stepmother was sitting regally upon a new ornate sofa. Noticing Ella's blotchy, tearstained face, she tilted her head and smiled. "Now, now. Mustn't blub." She motioned for Ella to come closer.

Grateful for this rare kind gesture, Ella sat next to her, giving her a quick embrace. "Yes, Stepmother."

"You needn't call me that," Lady Tremaine responded. Ella looked up hopefully. Was her stepmother starting to warm up to her? Perhaps she was growing friendlier due to the fact that they would both miss Father. "*Madam* will do."

Ah, Ella thought. *So much for that.*

Suddenly, a flurry of yellow and pink activity descended upon the hall adjacent to them.

"There isn't room for me and all of your clothes!" Drisella cried.

"Then make yourself smaller," Anastasia retorted. Their bickering continued and escalated to name-calling and vicious threats.

Ella's stepmother seemed undisturbed. "Anastasia and Drisella have always shared a room. Such dear, affectionate girls."

"Or better yet, disappear entirely!" came Anastasia's shrill scream.

"You'd like that, wouldn't you? Sometimes I could scratch your eyes out!" Drisella yelled.

Lady Tremaine examined her nails. "I think they're finding the quarters rather confining," she said by way of explanation.

Ella felt a twinge of guilt. The girls were put up in an awfully small room. And she had thought of sharing her room with the girls before they'd arrived. Now she was not exactly sure she'd want to stay *with* them. But that didn't mean they couldn't use it.

"My bedroom is the biggest besides yours and Father's," she said out loud. "Perhaps they would like to have it."

Lady Tremaine smiled at her, clearly pleased. "A wonderful suggestion. What a good girl you are."

Ella returned her smile. "I can stay in—"

"The attic," her stepmother finished. "Quite so."

Ella stared at her, confused. There were plenty of

other rooms in the home where she could go. "The attic?"

"Yes," Lady Tremaine said, waving off Ella's look of concern. "Just temporarily, of course, until I redecorate."

The woman reached for a box on the end table next to them. It contained some keepsakes from her father's travels, as well, Ella noticed, as the portrait of her mother. "And it would be even more cozy for you if you kept all of this bric-a-brac up there with you."

Ella took the box and held it closer to her chest, her mother's words echoing in her head. *Be kind.*

"You may take these as well," her stepmother continued, gesturing airily toward the books on the bookcases. "*Natural Philosophy, Mathematics, Histories.* These books are too *bookish* for me. They depress my spirits."

Ella suppressed the urge to giggle at this. Until, that is, she took a book from her stepmother and noticed something golden glinting on her hand. Her mother's ring. Sobered, Ella quickly looked up at Lady Tremaine, unsure of what to say. The woman stared at her and lifted her perfectly shaped eyebrows as though challenging her stepdaughter to react.

Ella looked down at her mother's portrait, gaining strength from the familiar kind face. *I will not forget my promise.*

"Madam," she said, giving a little curtsy before leaving her stepmother alone.

Ella looked up at the daunting wooden staircase. It appeared to go on forever. Most of the members of the house avoided the attic, primarily because of the crookedness and narrowness of the staircase, as well as the cold, uninviting space where it led.

After a deep breath, Ella eventually made it to the small curved door. She pushed it open.

The attic was larger than she'd remembered, and actually, beneath the dust and forgotten sheet-covered furniture, not as terrible as she had feared. There were windows overlooking the front of the house, and tiny glass panels on the far wall that let in sparkling squares of sunlight. Ella put her box of things down and smiled. This actually might do quite nicely.

Spotting a covered chaise longue against the far wall, Ella pushed it toward the center of the room. She fluffed up some pillows and arranged them artfully on her new bed. Then she gingerly sat down.

"Well, no one shall disturb me here," Ella said aloud. A sudden movement behind the chaise startled her. Spotting her mouse friends, she clapped her hands in delight.

"Oh! Hello, Jacqueline, hello, Gus. So this is where you take refuge. Me, too, it would seem."

The mice wiggled their whiskers at her.

"How very pleasant," Ella said, kicking her feet in front of her. "No cats and no stepsisters." She winked at the mice and then rose, heading over to the box she'd left on the other side of the room. She might as well unpack her things.

Suddenly, Ella tripped on a loose floorboard. "Oh!" she cried, steadying herself. Then she knelt, examining the board more closely. She lifted it to find a hollowed-out space. Ella had an idea.

"This will do *quite* nicely. Everyone needs a hiding place, you know," she told the mice. "For their secret things."

And in her special hiding place, Ella stowed her most prized possessions—the toy butterfly her father had given to her long ago, and the portrait of her mother.

Ella's great comfort during this time was the letters her father would send on his travels. One such letter arrived not too long after Ella had moved into the attic.

> *My dear Ella,*
>
> *How I miss you so. I saw a bright blue butterfly on the road today and it made me think of you. "And so we'll live / And pray, and sing, and tell old tales, and laugh / At gilded butterflies. . . ."* King Lear, *you know. But of course you do, my darling!*
>
> *I hope you are well, and that your stepmother and stepsisters are being just as kind as you are. And if they are not, which I fear is most likely the case, I hope they are not bothering you at the very least.*
>
> *I will be home in a few weeks yet, my dear, but do not fret. You are your mother's daughter. You have her strength and bravery as well as her goodness. I have no doubt that you will be fine while I am away.*
>
> *Please give my best to the staff as well. I very much hope each and every member of our household is well cared for and content while I am away.*
>
> *All my love,*
> *Father*

As Ella finished reading in the dim candlelight, she held the letter close to her heart, shivering in the drafty attic air. A few weeks to go. She missed her father terribly. She could not wait to talk with him, to hear his easy laugh, to share a new favorite passage from a book she'd read. His return could not come soon enough.

Time ticked by. And though she looked forward to her father's return, Ella grew resolved to make the most of every day. To focus on the things that made her happy, such as spending time with the staff, taking pleasure in helping keep the house running smoothly, and visiting with the animals she loved so much.

Every morning, Ella would rise with the rooster's cry, feeding the birds and the goats, milking the cows, and gathering some eggs for the kitchen.

She would often dip her finger in the simmering pots to have a taste of whatever delicious concoction Flora was whipping up, much to Flora's amusement as well as her chagrin.

She would visit the shepherd James and his flock, and help Helen with the mending and the cleaning, all the while chatting with Helen about her lovely niece and nephew.

Then Ella would help her stepfamily with whatever they needed that day: a cup of tea, a hand with corseting, setting up the easel for Anastasia's painting, or tuning the piano for Drisella's playing.

One afternoon, the girls were practicing their artistic endeavors in the drawing room, Drisella in mid-song and Anastasia with her sketchpad. Lady Tremaine oversaw the scene, perched from her favorite spot on the settee in the center of the room, while Ella busied herself with the tea tray. Lucifer, bored with the entire ordeal, sat stiffly under a table. He occasionally nodded off, just to be awoken by Drisella's dissonant chords.

"AhhhhhhhhhhHHHHHHhhhh." Drisella sang a particularly sharp note, causing Ella to flinch. She glanced down and saw that Jacqueline and Gus had their paws over their ears. She stifled a giggle.

"Look, Mother," Anastasia said, holding up her sketchpad. "It's you." To Anastasia's credit, the drawing did somewhat resemble Lady Tremaine in a few respects, though in an exaggerated and unflattering way, as though through a distorted mirror.

Lady Tremaine's eyes narrowed. "Yes, dear."

Once more, Ella tried to keep herself from laughing. She turned away.

Unfortunately, Lady Tremaine noticed her stepdaughter's amusement. Casting a devious eye at the girl, her stepmother lifted her cup of tea ever so gently, then dropped it, watching the cup bounce and fall and turn into shattered pieces. The ruddy liquid started to stain Ella's mother's favorite carpet.

"Oh, dear," Lady Tremaine said casually.

Hearing the clinking glass, Ella hurried over to clean up the mess, hoping there was not too much damage done.

From beneath the table, Lucifer shot her a smug look. Ella sighed as she cleaned. The Tremaines were certainly trying. *They do not know any other way. Have courage,* she reminded herself for not the first time that week, *and be kind.*

Chapter 6

FOR their part, the Tremaines seemed to find the house and its "quirks" vexing. Claiming that the country air exhausted them, Lady Tremaine and her daughters began to take their breakfasts in their respective rooms every morning.

Soon they were so "exhausted" that they could not get out of bed to eat their morning meal. They resorted to ringing the old servants' bells to signal that they needed something.

The first time Ella and Flora had heard the network of bells sounding in the kitchen, they'd jumped.

Looking at the startled expressions reflected in one another's faces, they began to laugh.

Flora put a hand to her heart. "Well, I, for one, am *much* too old for such frights."

"I almost threw all of the salt into the pot," Ella said.

The bells rang again, this time somehow sounding more insistent. Ella and Flora watched as dust flew off the copper, and the moth-eaten labels, which signaled which bell belonged to which room, began to crumble from the vibration. Ella had never known a time when those loud dreadful things had been used in the house. Judging by their state, they probably hadn't been rung in decades.

Flora's expression hardened. "It would seem we are being summoned by her *ladyship*."

Ella put a hand on the cook's shoulder. "I'll go." Picking up the tray brimming with tea, toast, cakes, and fruit, she made her way toward the door. Then, turning back to Flora, she added with a twinkle in her eye, "Besides, I for one cannot wait to see how she reacts to blueberries for the third morning in a row."

Flora laughed, playfully shaking a towel at her. "You are too good, Miss Ella. Too good."

Soon the Tremaines' lethargy began to extend through supper, tea, and dinner as well. They kept all of the members of the house busier than ever, ordering them to collect dresses from market, or paint a piece of furniture a new color to suit their whims.

When she wasn't helping the others sweep the floors or dust the furniture, Ella often found herself running from the kitchen to their rooms, their meals in tow.

Taking advantage of Ella's unfailing willingness to help, Lady Tremaine's requests grew exponentially. Ella would mend and wash the Tremaines' clothes, would fill their baths, and would even dress them in the mornings. She did not have a spare moment for herself. She couldn't remember the last time she had picked up a book or went for a ride or took a stroll through the meadow.

One day, a loud knocking interrupted her mopping. *Father!* Ella dropped the mop in excitement, and wiped her hands on her apron.

"At last!" she cried, hopping down the stairs two at a time. She swung the door open.

"I—" she stopped short, seeing Farmer John standing in front of her, a somber expression on his face. He held his hat against his heart. Ella frowned in confusion.

"It's your father, Miss Ella," John started, his voice shaking. "He took ill on the road."

Ella blinked at him, terrible understanding dawning on her.

"He's passed on, miss," Farmer John continued. "He's gone."

Ella heard a movement behind her. Lady Tremaine, Anastasia, and Drisella had gathered by the door. Ella's whole body began to tremble. She took a deep breath, trying to process John's words.

"To the end, he spoke of no one but you, miss. And your mother." John handed Ella a slender, leaf-lined branch. "I was to give this to you."

Ella turned the branch over in her hands, a frail piece of wood with its drying leaves, the last remnant of her father's devotion.

"But what about my lace?" Anastasia's shrill voice cut through the moment.

"My parasol?" Drisella joined in.

"Can't you see?" Lady Tremaine snapped. "None of that matters."

Ella turned, seeing her stepmother's ashen face. She seemed just as heartbroken as Ella. She had, after all, lost a husband for the second time. Ella suddenly felt moved at thought that her stepmother cared so deeply. Perhaps in this awful, dark hour, the two of them could reconcile their differences, could come together as a family.

"We're ruined!" her stepmother cried. "How will we live?" She put a hand over her face, walking away from the scene, her stepdaughters following her.

In that moment, Ella's grief overwhelmed her. She turned back to the open door, seeing Farmer John's crestfallen expression. Ella realized she was not the only one grieving.

"Thank you," she told him gently, her voice shaking. "That must have been very difficult for you." She reached out and touched his arm. John nodded wistfully. Then he turned, making his way back to the cart and horses.

Ella slowly closed the door and sank down against its sturdy wooden frame. The tears came freely. And this time, Ella did not try to stop them.

Chapter 7

THE first thing Lady Tremaine did after her husband's death was let the household staff go. Sacrifices needed to be made, she told them. Without someone providing for the family, they could not afford the luxury of a full staff.

Ella saw them off, these kind souls who had been as much a part of the house and family as her parents had been. She helped them pack and put their bags in the cart that was to whisk them away.

Giving each one a big hug, Ella whispered words of comfort, wiping their tears. Some of them had family to stay with, like Helen and her dear sister, niece, and nephew, but many of them had nowhere else to go. She hoped they would find employment elsewhere soon.

The staff, in turn, hoped that Ella's life, already

filled with so much heartache and tragedy, would get better.

"I will pray for you, sweet Miss Ella," the old shepherd James said. "You truly are your parents' daughter."

"Thank you, James," Ella told him, giving him a quick kiss on the cheek.

Ella saved her good-bye with Flora for last. The two looked at one another for a moment, tears brimming in their eyes.

They embraced, each trying to comfort the other.

"It will be all right," Ella said.

"There is no need to cry, my dear," Flora told her at the same time.

They looked at one another and laughed through the tears. Then, with one last hug, Flora joined the rest of the staff on the cart.

As Ella waved good-bye from her spot in front of the house, she took a deep breath. A new chapter was about to begin. And she would have to gather all her strength and courage to face it.

Despite the need to "make sacrifices," Lady Tremaine ordered the finest mourning gowns for herself and her two daughters made of fine black bombazine. Not surprisingly, she did not order one for Ella, but Ella did not mind. She preferred her blue frock, one that she had worn when her father was around. True, it was a bit old now, but Ella took great pains to clean and mend it.

Instead of a heavy black gown, Ella displayed her mourning with a black ribbon in her hair. Every time she tied it to her curls, she would think of her father and try to come up with a quote to accompany it, knowing he would appreciate such a ritual.

"'O time! Thou must untangle this, not I; / It is too hard a knot for me to untie!'" Ella let out a little laugh as she tightened the bow. *This will be too hard a knot for me this evening, I daresay.*

With the staff gone, the household duties fell entirely on Ella as her stepmother and stepsisters continued to lounge about each day. It was too much work for one person, but Ella knew she had to do what she could, lest her family's estate, her parents' cherished home, fall to ruins.

Moreover, as much as she hated to think of herself this way, Ella was now an orphan. And Lady Tremaine, the mistress of the home, clearly saw Ella as a dependent, an interloper, another mouth to feed in a home where the finances were quickly dwindling. Ella was expected to earn her keep. Otherwise, it was very likely she'd be ordered to leave like Flora and the rest of the staff had been.

Of course, this working role in the household did not come as a surprise to Ella. It had been clear for some time that the Tremaines did not see her as family. In fact, it renewed her sense of purpose. She would throw all her energy into caring for the house and the animals. And she would do so happily, kindly. For she had these wonderful things—the beautiful estate, the companionable creatures, in addition to scores of happy memories—all because of her parents. There were so many who did not have so much.

So Ella fetched the water from the well. She took care of the dusting and sweeping and mopping. She built the fires and prepared the meals. She polished the silver and cleaned the chamber pots. She did the laundry and the ironing and the mending. She harvested the fruits and vegetables and tended to the animals.

She answered the call of the servants' bells, which never seemed to stop ringing now. She made sure her stepsisters and her stepmother received everything they asked for. More importantly, she took pains to make sure the mice were okay, to make sure that Lucifer did not bother them. With Ella being busier than ever, she wanted to be sure that the pesky cat did not get to them when she wasn't looking.

All this, and more, she would do during the day

and into the wee hours of the night, most of the time singing a happy tune or reciting a favorite sonnet during her work.

"Lavender's green, dilly dilly," Ella sang one afternoon as she scrubbed a few bowls in soapy water.

RRRRRRRRRRINNNNNNNNNNNGGGG.

Ella looked up at the servants' bells. It appeared she was needed in Lady Tremaine's dressing room. Putting the bowl down, Ella wiped her hands on a towel, then headed up to her stepmother's quarters, unconsciously continuing her song.

"Lavender's blue, dilly dilly . . ."

"Will you please stop that incessant singing?" Lady Tremaine asked as Ella entered the room. "I have a headache."

"As you wish, madam," Ella replied, walking over to her.

Her stepmother held out an arm covered in a thick magenta sleeve. It had been a few weeks since she had donned her mourning gown, reverting back to colorful, expensive dresses that reflected the latest fashions.

Ella buttoned both sleeves at the wrist. Then, as Lady Tremaine pointedly placed a foot on top of a velvet stool, Ella bent down. She helped the woman ease her heel into the shiny boot, and started to tie the laces.

As Ella helped her stepmother dress, she noticed something in the corner of the room she hadn't seen before—her father's portrait, now sitting on a low table. It was tilted toward the wall, but she could still make out her father's winsome smile.

Ella looked up at Lady Tremaine and saw that the woman was staring at her. They looked at one another, the silence filled with so much.

"I—" Ella started to say. But her stepmother cut her off.

"If you are quite finished, there is some laundry that has been needed to be washed for days."

Ella stood up, keeping her gaze on her stepmother. She felt a rush of pity for this woman who had so much bitterness in her heart. Who kept the world, and even her own daughters, at arm's length.

"Yes, madam," Ella said, exiting the room.

To their credit, it should be said that the Tremaines shared the food they ate with Ella. And Ella shared it in turn with her mouse friends, Jacqueline and Gus, and their children, Jacob and Esau. As Ella didn't really have any other friends to speak of now, she invested the littlest creatures with spirit, and opened her heart to them.

"There you are!" Ella said as the four mice crept quietly into the candlelit kitchen. It had been a long day of chores, and the clock had just struck three in the morning. "Have dinner with me, won't you?"

She emptied the leftover food from her step-mother's and stepsisters' plates onto another. Placing a teacup upside down, Ella rested a saucer over it. Then, spotting a small lace doily, she laid it across the top.

"Your table," Ella said, presenting it to the mice, who scurried up to it. She took a crust of bread off of her plate, and sprinkled the crumbs on the little table for the mice. These makeshift dinners were becoming part of Ella's nightly routine. She enjoyed making them more and more festive.

"Cheers," she said as the mice twitched their noses at her. Ella winked at them. Then, at long last, she sat down and began to eat her scraps.

A sudden lethargy hit her as she ate. Her eyes felt heavy, and she felt herself nod off once or twice during her meal. Soon Ella felt as though she would fall asleep face down on her plate.

"I believe it is time for bed," she announced, putting her dish away.

But once she got to the bottom of the daunting

staircase that led up to the attic, Ella shook her head. The never-ending twists and turns looked practically insurmountable in that moment, and the attic's cool draft was already cutting down at her with its icy wind.

Ella decided she would not make it up to her room that night. Instead, she would head back to the kitchen hearth for warmth. That would be much more pleasant.

Soon Ella was lying down near the dying embers, the mice curled up at her feet. All five of them, the four wee mice and the sweet young woman, immediately drifted off to a dreamless sleep.

RRRRRRRRRRINNNNNNNNNNGGGG.

Ella woke with a start. She hurried to start the kettle for tea and arrange the food she'd prepared yesterday for breakfast. Her stepfamily had started to take their meals in the drawing room, and expected everything in order by the time they came down.

Hearing creaks from upstairs, Ella rushed to the drawing room, shifting a blanket to cover the worn headrest on one of the chairs, reminding herself to sew a patch on the torn settee.

She was just adding a log to the fire when Lady

Tremaine, Anastasia, and Drisella breezily entered the room.

"I thought breakfast was ready," her stepmother said, looking at the barren table.

"It is, madam," Ella replied. "I am only mending the fire."

Lady Tremaine tutted impatiently. "In the future, can we not be called until the work is done?"

Ella did not remind her that she had not called them at all. "As you wish," she said, collecting the breakfast tray from the kitchen. She started to serve the tea when her stepmother issued another pointed remark.

"What is that on your face?"

Ella's hand flew to her cheek. ". . . Madam?"

"It's ash from the fireplace!" Anastasia cried with glee.

Her stepmother surveyed her a bit more, her cheeks twitching. "Clean yourself up." In her scolding, Lady Tremaine could not keep the delight out of her voice at seeing Ella in such a state. "You'll get cinders in our tea."

Drisella clapped her hands. "I've got a name for her. Cinderwench!"

Lady Tremaine laughed as Ella tried to ignore them, serving the rest of the breakfast.

"I couldn't *bear* to look so dirty," Anastasia announced as she took a bite of toast. Then her eyes lit up. *"Oooh! Dirty Ella!"*

"Cinderella!" Drisella practically shouted, clearly proud of herself. "That's what we'll call you!"

Lady Tremaine chuckled approvingly. "You're *too* clever," she told her daughter.

Ella wore a polite smile, setting her plate and teacup down at the empty chair.

Lady Tremaine narrowed her eyes. "Who's this for? Is there someone we've forgotten?"

Ella smiled wanly, looking from her stepmother to her stepsisters. This was clearly another one of their hurtful games. "It's my place."

"It seems too much to expect you to prepare breakfast, serve it, and still sit with us," Lady Tremaine said. "Wouldn't you prefer to eat when all the work is done, Ella?" She shot a glance at her daughters. "Or should I say, 'Cinderella'?"

She clasped her hands together demurely, and Ella could once again see her mother's ring, the ruby sparkling in the morning light.

For Ella, this was the last straw, the breaking point. Her hands shaking as she picked up her plate, she hurried out of the room, not wanting to give the Tremaines the satisfaction of seeing her cry.

She tried to set the plate gently down on the kitchen table, but her hands were trembling too much. The plate fell to the floor, shattering into tiny pieces. Tears stinging her eyes, Ella knelt down to clean up the mess when something caught her eye.

It was her reflection in a shiny copper pot. But this was not the Ella she knew. No, this was a thin, dirty girl, her hair knotted and dull, all the light and hope extinguished from her eyes. This was somebody different entirely.

"Names have power," she thought back to what James the shepherd had said long ago.

How right that is, she thought. *For I am no longer the happy little girl I was with Mother and Father. No, it is clear I am changed.*

I am Cinderella.

INDERELLA

Chapter 8

LLA, now Cinderella, took deep breaths, trying to steady herself. She had only felt so overwhelmed one other time in her life. And suddenly, she knew what she had to do. She had to get outside.

Cinderella ran to the stables, feeling grateful that her stepmother had seen the benefits of keeping at least one horse. Galahad neighed a worried whinny when he saw her, sensing her despair.

Cinderella knew that riding in the countryside, away from her stepfamily, would be the only way to to clear her mind of the morning's events.

Galahad pranced about in his stall. It was clear she was not the only one eager for a ride.

Soon they were off. Cinderella felt the anger and the pain melt away with every hoofbeat. She let

Galahad go where he pleased, and he led them past her favorite spots—the meadow now overgrown with purple wildflowers, the babbling brook that seemed to be singing, the clump of tall trees that marked the beginning of the forest.

Cinderella took deep gulps of the cool fresh air and felt the rays of sunlight peering through the trees warm her face. Ella had missed the freedom of riding. She realized she hadn't ridden like this for years, since before the Tremaines had come into their lives.

Suddenly, Galahad reared, almost throwing Cinderella to the ground. "Whoa, boy, whoa," she said, patting his mane soothingly. She looked up at what had spooked him.

It was a mighty stag, an apparition of the forest itself. He stood proudly, his gigantic antlers gleaming, his front hooves ready to flee at a moment's notice. Cinderella locked eyes with the magnificent creature, and felt a profound moment of calm. It was almost as if the stag were reminding her that all would be well.

At that moment, the call of a trumpet interrupted them. Cinderella heard approaching hoof-steps, and realization dawned on her. There was a hunt nearby.

"Run!" she told the stag. "Go, quickly!"

The stag bolted into the trees. Galahad, frightened by the sudden movement, followed suit, sprinting haphazardly through the foliage.

"Whoa, Galahad," Cinderella said, trying to calm him. "Whoa, boy."

The trees were much closer together this deep in the forest. Cinderella directed Galahad this way and that, desperately trying to avoid a crash.

Just then, another rider appeared, grabbing Galahad's reins from atop his dark steed and slowing Cinderella's horse to a trot.

Cinderella frowned, glancing up at the stranger who'd helped her. He was a young man with dark wavy hair and clear blue eyes. His handsome face was filled with concern. Their horses circled one another as though they, too, were sizing each other up.

"Are you all right?" the stranger asked breathlessly.

Cinderella almost laughed. What a question. "I'm all right, but you nearly frightened the life out of *him*."

The man looked from her to Galahad, who seemed calm enough now. "Who?" he asked.

She smiled. He looked ever so grave. "The stag," she told him. "What has he ever done to you that you should chase him about?"

"I confess I've never met him before," the man said, surprised. "He is a friend of yours?"

"An acquaintance," Cinderella explained. "We met just now. I looked into his eyes, and he looked into mine, and I felt he had a great deal to do with his life. That's all."

The man returned her smile, his eyes twinkling. "Miss—what do they call you?"

The question struck a nerve. Cinderella looked down, feeling her face flush with embarrassment. "Never mind what they call me."

"You shouldn't be this deep in the forest alone," he said as she took Galahad's reins from him.

Again, Cinderella suppressed a laugh. She was by far happier and safer here deep in the forest than she had been at home for quite some time. Besides, she had Galahad and the majestic stag and . . . and now this young man for company.

"I'm not alone," she replied. "I'm with you, Mr.— what do they call you?"

"You don't know who—that is," the man faltered, seeming just as embarrassed as she had moments ago. "They call me Kit. Well, my father does, when he's in a good mood."

Cinderella smiled encouragingly, hoping to put Kit at ease. "Where do you live, Mr. Kit?"

"Oh, I live at the palace," he answered. "My father is teaching me his trade."

"You're an apprentice!" Cinderella exclaimed. She'd always been impressed by those learning a trade, contributing something to the world. "That is very fine. Do they treat you well?"

Kit laughed. "Better than I deserve, most likely. And you?"

Cinderella answered truthfully, shaking her head. "They treat me as well as they are able."

Kit leaned forward on his horse, the concern once again apparent in his kind eyes.

"I'm sorry."

"It's not your doing," she said.

"Not yours either, I'll bet."

Cinderella looked away, uncomfortable with the direction of the conversation. "It's not so very bad. Others have it worse, I'm sure," she said, meaning it. "We must simply have courage and be kind, mustn't we?"

Kit seemed at once baffled and impressed by her words. He leaned back, as if mulling them over a few times.

". . . Yes. You're right. That's exactly how I feel." He, again, sounded surprised.

The braying of the horns sounded once more. It seemed the other hunters were on their way.

Cinderella felt a surge of panic. "Please don't let them hurt him!" She could not stand the thought of that beautiful creature suffering, particularly for sport.

This time Kit knew exactly who she was talking about. "But . . . we're *hunting*, you see," he said slowly. "It's what's done."

"Just because it's what's done, doesn't mean it's what *should* be done," Cinderella countered.

Kit examined her face more closely, intrigued. "Right again."

She lowered her voice. "Then you'll leave him alone, won't you?" she asked gently.

He looked at her very seriously. "Yes, all right," he agreed.

"Thank you very much, Mr. Kit," Cinderella said, relieved.

They looked at one another shyly. Cinderella was about to speak again when they heard peals of the hunting horn just behind them.

A man in a blue uniform rode up to them on his own large steed. "Your—"

"It's me, *Kit.* It's Kit! I'm Kit," Kit sputtered.

Cinderella looked at him, amused. Could such a charming person be nervous?

"I'm on my way," Kit continued to call to the man in blue.

The man in blue simply grinned and nodded. Kit turned back to Cinderella.

"I hope I will see you again, miss."

Cinderella nodded. She found him quite sweet. ". . . And I, you."

Kit returned her smile, seemingly relieved that this was her answer.

The horns blared insistently, and Kit nodded to Cinderella once more before galloping off.

Cinderella watched him and the man in blue go, a small, thoughtful smile resting on her lips.

Cinderella and Galahad rode to the old familiar spot on the top of the hill. She looked down at the house, which, from here, looked as it always had—vibrant, calm, beautiful.

She thought about her stepfamily, about being called Cinderella, about her pleasant afternoon and her encounter with the charming stranger named Kit. A gentle breeze blew through her hair. The scent of daisies wafted around her, reminding Ella of her mother.

It was true—she had changed since her parents were alive. But she was proud of the way she had saved the stag from the hunt. She was proud of how hard she worked to keep the house. She was even proud of how she maintained her composure with her stepfamily.

Yes, she was no longer Ella. Her experiences had changed her, and she had grown into Cinderella.

But she suddenly realized that she liked who that person was. A person who still valued kindness and courage more than anything. A person who would stick up for what was right. A person who believed that goodness had power.

And she knew her parents would have liked that person, too.

K IT

Chapter 9

KIT was silent for the majority of the ride back to the palace. His friend, the Captain of the Guard, kept stealing sidelong glances at him, an amused expression on his face.

He suspected the Captain had an idea of what had made him announce to the other men that the hunting trip was over for the day. And furthermore, that he would not be going on any more hunting trips in the future.

"Just because it's what's done, doesn't mean it's what should be done," she'd said.

What an amazing statement. So pure, so simple. Why hadn't *he* thought of that? And why hadn't he said something similar whenever he felt uncomfortable by how things were done, such as how war always seemed to be seen as a good solution? Or how he was expected to marry immediately? Or even how mutton had to be served at every meal? Really, it was such an unpleasant dish.

Kit grinned at his own stupidity. He wished he'd said something like that to the girl in the woods. To show her that he agreed with her sentiments whole-heartedly. And to show her that he could be funny. No one ever expected him to be funny.

But on second thought, perhaps that was because he *wasn't* funny. He decided if he ever did see the girl again, and oh, how he hoped he would, he would forgo any joking whatsoever.

Just then, the trumpets blared from behind him, announcing the group's return to the palace. Kit sighed as they rode through the open gates and over the drawbridge. The taupe stone walls, as well as the hundreds of windows that covered them, gleamed in the sunlight. The opulent Grecian statues seemed to look at Kit as he passed them, welcoming him home.

A stable boy approached, reaching for Kit's reins.

"It's all right," Kit told the boy. "I can take him in myself. I'd like to give him some extra sugar cubes." He patted the horse affectionately. "Guildenstern, here, has earned a treat."

The boy ducked his head apologetically. "I'm sorry, I am to tell you that you are wanted in the king's quarters." He bowed lower, bending at the waist. "Your Highness."

"You sound as if you're the first fellow who ever met a pretty girl," King Frederick said teasingly.

Kit sat next to his father on a small sofa. The royal physician was rolling up the king's sleeve, performing his increasingly frequent exams on the ruler.

"She wasn't 'a pretty girl,'" Kit said. Then, seeing his father's look, he grinned. "Well, she was a pretty girl. But there was so much more to her."

King Frederick's eyes widened. "How much more? You've only met her once. How can you know anything about her?"

"You told me you knew right away when you met Mother," Kit countered.

The doctor took another tool out of his bag, listening for the king's heartbeat.

"That's different. Your mother was a princess."

Kit shook his head. "You would have loved her anyway."

King Frederick shifted closer to his son. "I would never have met her because it wouldn't have been appropriate. And my father, rest his bones, would have told me what I'm telling you, and *I* would have listened."

Kit laughed jovially. "No, you wouldn't."

"Yes, I would."

"No, you wouldn't."

"No, I wouldn't," the king finally admitted, laughing with his son.

At that moment, the doctor rolled King Frederick's sleeve down and started to put his equipment away.

Kit stood to address the man. "How is he?"

There was a brief silence as the doctor tried to find the words.

The king nodded. "Never mind," he told the royal physician. "If it takes that long to work out a way to say it, I already know it's bad."

Kit sank back down on the sofa next to his father, his face stricken, all the lightness and play of the room suddenly turned serious. "Father . . ."

Patting his son's arm, King Frederick smiled wistfully. "It's the way of all flesh, boy." Then he stood. "Come. We will be late. And . . ." He nodded his head toward Kit, who grinned, knowing what his father was about to say.

"Punctuality is the politeness of princes," they said in unison, the two breaking into chuckles once more. But behind his outward good humor, Kit felt a pang of worry for his father.

King Frederick and his son started down the hallway, and were soon joined by the Captain of the Guard and the Grand Duke, a stout man with a bushy mustache.

"My King, Your Highness," the Duke greeted them, falling into step with the others. Then he nodded at the prince. "I am sure your father spoke to you of your behavior in the forest."

"Is it any business of yours, Grand Duke?" Kit asked.

"My business is your business, Your Highness," the Grand Duke answered smoothly. "It will not do to let the stag go free."

The four men turned the corner, heading down another refined hallway lined with curved windows and polished sculptures.

"Just because it's what's done, doesn't mean it's what *should* be done," the prince answered. "Something like that."

The king patted his son on the back. "Still the dreamer. I had hoped that a bit of campaigning would knock some sense into you." Then, tilting his head back, he asked, "What have you got to say, Captain?"

The Captain smiled, reflecting on those months spent away with the prince. "I'd say the war knocked some common sense *out* of him, sir. While I have never seen a fellow more brave, he exhibited a very troubling tendency to think."

King Frederick paused before responding good-naturedly. "Sometimes I fear for this kingdom."

Kit laughed as they reached their destination—the salon, a large room with high ceilings that was filled with props, benches, easels, paints, and brushes. This was where all the royal portraits and paintings were completed.

The royal portraitist sat in front of a large half-finished canvas, impatiently tapping his foot. He was a fussy, senile chap, who had the unfortunate tendency to say whatever was on his mind.

"Make him look *marriageable,* Master Phineas," the king told the man as they entered. "We must attract a suitable bride, even if he is a terrible dunce."

"I shall endeavor to please, Your Highness," Master Phineas responded, dipping his brush in paint. "But I can't work bloody miracles," he added.

Kit exchanged a look with his father. "I see Master Phineas is alive and well."

"For our sins," the king responded as Kit took his place on the mocked-up saddle at the head of the room.

The portraitist was creating a life-size canvas that would show Kit astride a tall steed, a sword in his hand as though he were charging into battle. Kit did not think it was exactly the best representation of who he was, and it was quite a difficult pose to hold. But he had to admit, he enjoyed listening to Master Phineas's colorful commentary.

"A splendid canvas, Master Phineas," the Captain remarked.

"Thank you, Your Grace. As if he knows anything about art," the portraitist said in the same breath.

"So these portraits will be sent abroad?" Kit asked.

"Yes, if you can convince a princess of sufficient rank that you are *not* a dunderhead, we may secure a powerful alliance," King Frederick responded playfully.

"At this ball you and the Grand Duke insist upon."

The Grand Duke interjected. "At which you will choose a bride. We are a small kingdom amongst great states, Your Highness. And it is a dangerous world. We must get what allies we can."

Kit shifted the sword in his hand, prompting a soft cry of alarm from Master Phineas. "I feel like a prize pig being sold at market."

"Some prize," the portraitist muttered.

"If I must marry, why would I not wed . . . say, a good, honest country girl?" Kit asked.

The Grand Duke guffawed. "And how many divisions of infantry would this 'good, honest country girl' provide us?"

At that moment, the king walked closer to Kit, his

face serious. He lowered his voice as he addressed his son. "I would like to see you—and the kingdom—safe and secure."

Kit immediately grasped his meaning. His father was not well. He wanted to make sure everything was settled before he left this world. Kit reached out to touch his father's arm, much to Master Phineas's dismay. Out of the corner of his eye, he saw the portraitist throw his brush in the air in exasperation.

"All right," the prince announced to the room. "I will agree to the ball. But let the invitations go to everyone, not just the nobility. The wars have brought sorrow enough."

King Frederick walked back across the room to the Captain. "What do you think? Would it please the people?"

"It's beyond my wit, Your Highness," the Captain replied. "But I wouldn't mind a bit of jolly."

The Grand Duke interjected once again, his booming voice filled with pleasure. "I think we may have struck a bargain. A ball for the people, a princess for the prince."

The prince's bright eyes met the Duke's beady ones. He nodded. "Agreed."

INDERELLA

Chapter 10

THOUGH her living conditions were much the same, things had gotten significantly better since Cinderella's revelation atop the hill. She once again made a point to find the joy in every day, whether it was in playing a little game with her mouse friends or in harmonizing with the singing sparrows outside.

The days she went to town became her favorite days. Not only did she get to ride Galahad there and back, but she also got to meander through the hustle and bustle of the square, hearing the little conversations between vendors and customers as well as between old friends, smelling the sweet aroma of breads and spices and fruits for sale.

That was where Cinderella found herself now, wandering between the wares of the fishmonger and the flower seller.

"If it isn't Miss Ella," a voice called from behind her. Cinderella turned to see her old friend, the family's former cook. "Flora!" she cried, embracing the woman.

Leaning back to inspect her, Cinderella was happy to see that Flora looked much the same—her cheeks round and rosy. "Are you well?" Cinderella asked. "Have you found employment?"

"Can anyone roast a chicken better, I ask you?" Flora responded in her familiar manner. Then her jolly face darkened. "You don't look well, miss, not at all. Why do you stay there when they treat you so?"

Cinderella answered the question truthfully. "I made Mother and Father a promise to cherish the place where they were so happy. They loved our house, and now that they are gone, I love it for them. So it's my home, you see."

Flora nodded, gently patting Cinderella's arm.

Suddenly, the blare of a trumpet cut through the chatter of the square, interrupting the reunion.

Flora and Cinderella turned to see the royal crier perched on a wooden stand nearby. He readied himself to make a royal pronouncement while a crowd gathered round.

"Hear ye! Hear ye! Know that our good King Frederick, fourth of that name, Protector of the Realm, Holy Elector of Thuringia, Sire of the Imperial Purple . . ." He went on listing the king's multitude of titles. The crowd started to stir, clearly growing rest-less. ". . . has decided that on this day two weeks hence there shall be held, at the palace, a royal ball. At said ball, in accordance with ancient custom, the prince shall choose a bride."

The crier looked up as the crowd murmured in excitement. Then he cleared his throat.

"Furthermore, at the behest of the prince, it is hereby declared that *every maiden in the kingdom*, be she noble or commoner, is invited to attend."

At this, the murmurs turned into full-fledged exclamations. This was completely unprecedented. Commoners had never been invited to royal balls before, much less a ball so important to the future of the kingdom.

Cinderella couldn't help but feel a rush of excite-ment. *Kit* lived at the palace, and as an apprentice there, would surely be in attendance. Perhaps she would see him there. Ever since the day they'd met in the for-est, she'd found her thoughts wandering to the sweet young man. She'd hoped that perhaps she would run into him again someday, though she'd known the odds were not likely. And now here was the perfect oppor-tunity to become better acquainted!

"It was so very nice to see you again, Flora," she said, giving the cook a quick hug. "But I'm afraid I must go!"

Forgetting all about the supplies she'd originally come to town for, Cinderella hopped on Galahad and hurried home straightaway. She was so excited she felt she had to tell *someone* the news about the ball, even if that someone was part of her stepfamily. Otherwise, she would burst.

Cinderella found the Tremaines where she'd left them that morning, lounging about in the drawing room. She rushed in and breathlessly relayed the royal crier's announcement. Much to Cinderella's delight, her stepsisters seemed as thrilled by the news as she was.

Clapping their hands with glee, they jumped up from their couches. It was only when they spoke that Cinderella realized their enthusiasm did not stem from simply being invited to the palace.

"I shall trick him into loving me, see if I don't!" Drisella proclaimed.

"This is the most hugeous news!" Anastasia said as she headed over to the mirror to fluff her curls.

Lady Tremaine slapped her hand on the arm of her chair, much like a judge would use a gavel. "Calm yourselves," she said sternly. "Listen to me."

All three young ladies looked at her. But it was clear Lady Tremaine was only talking to her daughters. "One of you must win the heart of the prince. Do that, and we can unwind the debt in which we were ensnared when we came to this backwater."

Cinderella's back stiffened at the insult.

"I, a *princess!*" Drisella cried, propelling herself into a frenzy all over again.

Not to be outdone, Anastasia interjected, turning back to her reflection. "Or rather, *I*, a princess!"

Suddenly, Lady Tremaine directed her attention at Cinderella. "Having delivered your news, why are you still here? You must return to town right away, and tell that seamstress to run up three fine ball gowns."

Cinderella was taken aback. She was surprised—and deeply touched—to think her stepmother would order a new dress for her as well as her own daughters. "Three? That is . . . very thoughtful of you."

"What do you mean?" Her stepmother narrowed her eyes.

"To think of me," Cinderella replied cautiously.

"Think of you?"

Drisella started to cackle from behind her mother. "Mummy, she believes the other dress is for *her.*" She started to walk toward Cinderella. "Poor, slow little Cinders. How *embarrassing.*"

Lady Tremaine appeared to be shocked. "You are too ambitious for your own good," she told her step-daughter. "Or mine."

Cinderella shook her head, trying to explain that unlike Drisella and Anastasia, she had no intention of wooing the prince. "But I only want to see my friend—"

Her stepmother rose, glaring down at Cinderella. "Let me be very clear," she spoke slowly, pointedly. "One gown for Drisella, one for Anastasia, and one for me. *À la mode Parisienne.*"

"She doesn't know what that means," Anastasia sneered.

"*Mais, bien sûr je connais la môde Parisienne et je vais faire mon meilleure au démissioner,*" Cinderella replied in perfect French.

The Tremaines gaped at her. Cinderella tried to hide her satisfaction at seeing them so shocked. But on the inside, she was delighted. *They certainly weren't expecting that.*

Attempting to recover her composure, Lady Tremaine started to speak once more. "Good. Right. That's settled then." She suddenly raised her voice. "Now go! Every bit of baggage in the kingdom will be tilting at the prince. You must get there first before the seamstress is drowning in work!"

KIT

Chapter 11

THE palace bustled with activity in preparation for the royal ball. With the addition of the commoners on the guest list, they were expecting upward of three hundred attendees. Every day, new stores of supplies were brought in, from barrels of wine to parcels containing the finest linens that would soon be sewn into tablecloths and liners. There were even boxes of fireworks, which would be set off at the start of the ball to commemorate the occasion.

Kit tried his best to stay out of the way, and, more importantly, to avoid the Grand Duke and his insistence that Kit learn the names, habits, and preferences of all the princesses who would be attending.

Kit escaped the madness in the palace's vast gardens. He often liked to walk the paths lined with perfectly sculpted hedges, past the marble basins and the tinkling fountains.

Nodding to one of the gardeners who was headed in the opposite direction, Kit noticed a hedge in the shape of a grand buck, rearing back on its hind legs. He paused in front of it, smiling and thinking, for not the first time that day, of the girl from the forest. How he hoped she would come.

The trouble was, of course, she did not know he was the prince. At first, this had pleased him. Finally, a person who would speak her mind in front of him. Someone who would not be thinking of his title.

But as the night of the ball approached, he wondered if his not telling her had been the right decision. She might be upset that he had not been entirely forthright. Or she might skip the ball entirely, not knowing that he had altered the terms specifically so that he might see her there.

Suddenly, he heard a familiar voice wafting toward him. "Have you seen His Royal Highness?" the Grand Duke asked. "He is supposed to be learning about the Princess Chelina of Zaragosa."

Not waiting to hear the reply, Kit quickly strode through the vine-covered archway in front of him. He looked around before pushing a nondescript wooden door and ducking his head to enter. *That wretched Duke will not find me* here.

"Here" was his favorite place in the palace—his mother's secret garden. It was a lush, colorful spot, overgrown with weeds and wildflowers from years of disuse, but all the more enchanting for it.

Kit made his way to the bench swing that still hung from a large oak. He sat down, making little indentations in the grass with his shoe.

When his mother had died all those years ago, Kit had tried to convince his father to accompany him on his frequent visits to the garden. But his father could not bring himself to do so. He missed his late wife too much to be so heavily reminded of her, of how much she'd adored swinging under the tree when they'd first wed, of the picnics they'd taken there as a family.

Kit smiled at the memory of the picnics. His parents had loved each other very much, a fact obvious to all who had known them, even the subjects they ruled over. He just hoped he could be afforded the same luxury when the time came for him to wed.

"Wake up, Your Highness," the Captain said, pointing his sword at Kit's arm. "You're in a daze."

Kit laughed, shaking his head. He realized that mid fencing practice was not the time to find oneself daydreaming.

"I'm sorry," he said, gathering himself and driving

his sword forward. The prince and the Captain were in one of the palace's great salons, practicing their swordsmanship amongst numerous other pairs of dueling partners. The salon echoed with the clang of swords and tapping of quick footwork.

"You've been off since the hunt." The Captain clashed his sword with the prince's.

"It's the girl," Kit replied, countering the Captain's move. "I've never met anyone like her."

"There are plenty of girls."

"But her spirit, her goodness . . ." Kit insisted.

The pair stopped, the conversation taking over Kit's concentration.

"I don't suppose she has a sister," the Captain said.

Kit laughed. "I don't know. I don't know anything about her!"

"Well, perhaps your mysterious girl will come to the ball," the Captain said. "That is why you threw the doors open, is it not?"

The prince feigned indignation. "Captain! It was for the benefit of the people."

"Of course." The Captain smiled. "How shallow of me."

"And if she comes? Then what?" Kit asked, voicing his fears aloud for the first time.

"Then you will tell her that you are the prince. And the prince may choose whichever bride he wants."

Kit looked at the Captain pointedly. "Ha." Then he resumed fencing, lifting his sword and taking a few quick steps forward.

"'Ha'?" the Captain echoed, moving backward.

"Yes, *ha*. You know my father and the Grand Duke will only have me marry a princess."

The Captain gave a flourished move to switch their direction. He swung his sword from side to side, now driving the play. "If this girl from the forest is as charming as you say, they may change their minds."

"Father might understand. But the Grand Duke— no," Kit replied.

They fenced in silence for a beat, the clanking of their swords echoing in the cavernous hall. Then the Captain spoke. "Well, there is always a way. You are a wily fellow, after all." He lunged toward the prince, who dodged and turned.

"And the king's wishes?" Kit asked.

"He's a good man, and a good king," the Captain said, reiterating what Kit already knew. "If he knows that you will rule the people fairly and keep the kingdom strong and the people happy, he will approve."

Kit smiled, a twinkle in his eye. "Then I pray you are wiser than you look," he said, advancing.

CINDERELLA

Chapter 12

AT long last, the day of the ball arrived. During the past week, Cinderella had been getting little to no sleep. She'd complete her household duties at about midnight, and would then spend a few hours working on her dress by candlelight.

It was her mother's—made of a beautiful blush-pink soft chiffon. It had needed only a little hemming and some repairing here and there. Otherwise, it fit her perfectly. She'd finished it just that morning at sunrise. Though she should have been exhausted, Cinderella felt a thrill of excitement when she thought of the dress and the ball to which she would wear it. She couldn't wait to run upstairs and put it on.

But there were others she needed to get ready first.

"Tighter!" Drisella cried as Cinderella pulled the string of her corset. "Tighter! *Agh!*"

Cinderella stopped, afraid she had hurt the girl. But Drisella uttered a breathless "Enough," motioning for Cinderella to tie up the corset. Cinderella sincerely hoped Drisella would not pass out from the lack of oxygen.

Anastasia clucked her tongue impatiently, and Cinderella walked to the other side of the sisters' room. She helped a flailing Anastasia into the structured hoop slip that would give her dress its wide bell shape. Anastasia kept telling Cinderella that she was putting the wooden slip on all wrong, abruptly shifting her torso left and right to observe Cinderella's work.

After narrowly missing being jabbed by Anastasia's pointy elbows, Cinderella managed to get her stepsister strapped in. She couldn't help thinking how her sisters' accessories resembled medieval torture devices. She hoped that they would be at least somewhat comfortable that evening.

After an hour of putting on more slips, stockings, and dresses, of curling and pinning, of painting and rouging, Anastasia and Drisella sized each other up while Cinderella started to straighten up the room.

They wore similar ensembles, Anastasia's a vibrant magenta covered in garish golden flowers, and Drisella's a lively yellow covered in clashing blue tulle. They each wore bright bows in their hair and held fans in their satin-gloved hands.

"A vision, Sister," Anastasia said through clenched teeth. "Truly."

"Likewise," Drisella replied, nodding at her.

Anastasia skipped to her vanity, pouting her lips out at her reflection. "We must not compete for the prince's hand. Let it not mean we harbor dark thoughts against each other."

"Of course, dear sister," Drisella said darkly, studying her fan. "I would not *dream* of poisoning you before we leave for the ball."

"Or I of dashing your brains out on the palace steps as we arrive." Anastasia turned, giving a sweet smile. "We are sisters, after all."

Drisella returned her smile. "We shall let the prince decide."

Now quite used to the sisters' rather morbid way of bickering, Cinderella was not bothered. She continued to tidy up the mess the girls had made in their pursuit of beauty. She was, however, curious about this prince she'd heard so much about. "What will he be like, I wonder."

"*Like?*" Anastasia repeated incredulously. She laughed. "What does it matter? He's rich beyond reason!"

Cinderella frowned. "Would you not like to know a bit about him before you marry him?"

"Certainly not!" Drisella interjected. "It might change my mind!"

Cinderella sighed, shaking her head as she returned to her task. She could not imagine being so intent on marrying someone she had never met, someone she had never even had a conversation with.

Noticing Cinderella's solemn expression, Anastasia skipped over to stepsister. "I bet you've never even *spoken* to a man. Have you, moon-face?"

Cinderella looked up. "I have. Once. To a gentleman . . ." A vision of Kit's handsome face appeared in her mind.

"Some *menial*, no doubt," Anastasia said, now dancing around the room, presumably practicing her waltz. "Some *prentice*."

"He was an apprentice, yes," Cinderella replied.

Drisella joined her sister's energetic dance. "All men are fools. That's what Mama says. The sooner you learn that, the better."

Cinderella stared at her sisters dancing about, listened to their plans to entrap the prince upon entering the ballroom. Not for the first time, she felt pity for these two schemers. With such a sad outlook on life and love, they would never experience what Cinderella hoped she might, something her parents had had—a pure, genuine, unselfish love.

Cinderella gazed upon her reflection in the cracked mirror. She tied in her hair the leftover pink fabric she'd made into ribbons, smiling as that familiar quotation floated through her head:

"O time! thou must untangle this, not I; / It is too hard a knot for me to untie!"

Putting her arms down, she squinted at herself. In this dress, with her hair tied back this way, she looked more like her mother than ever. It was truly remarkable.

She took a few steps to the loose floorboard. Lifting it, Cinderella surveyed her treasures, gently gliding a finger over the toy butterfly's soft wings and the worn portrait of her mother.

"I know you will both be with me tonight," she whispered. "It's not every day a girl gets to go to a ball."

Suddenly, Cinderella heard the loud voices of her stepfamily downstairs. She knew she'd better hurry or else they would surely leave her behind.

She raced down the attic stairs, a few at a time, and reached the top of the main staircase.

"I daresay no one in the kingdom will outshine my daughters," her stepmother was saying. She was in a dress of fine satin the color of a grass snake. Lavish jewels shined from her neck and ears, and a single feather adorned her smooth auburn hair.

Hearing the movement above, Lady Tremaine

looked up. Her eyes darkened. "Cinderella?" she asked in a voice as cold as ice.

Cinderella hurried down a few steps to explain. "It cost you nothing. It's my mother's old dress, you see. And I took it up myself." She lifted the hem of her dress to demonstrate.

From her place in the foyer, Drisella burst into peals of laughter. "Oh, la! *Cinderella* at the *ball!* No one wants a *servant* for a bride!"

Lady Tremaine, however, was as serious as Cinderella had ever seen her. She strode toward her, stopping her stepdaughter from climbing down the last few steps. "After all I've done—feeding you, clothing you, resisting every impulse to turn you out of doors—you try to . . . to *embarrass me* in front of the court?"

"I . . ." Cinderella blinked in surprise. "I don't want to embarrass you. I'm not going in order to meet the prince—"

"There's no question of your going at all," Lady Tremaine said, interrupting her.

Cinderella paused, trying to think of the words that would convince her stepmother to let her join them. "But all of the maidens in the land are invited. By order of the king."

Lady Tremaine threw her hands up. "It is the *king* I am thinking of. It would be an insult to the royal personage to take you to the palace in those old rags."

"Rags?" Cinderella looked down. "This was my mother's."

Something inside Lady Tremaine seemed to snap in that moment. She leaned in, her face inches from her stepdaughter's. "Since you mention her in my house, you thoughtless girl, I can tell you that your mother's taste was questionable."

Cinderella felt as though she'd been struck. She opened her mouth to say something—anything—but her stepmother wasn't finished.

"This . . . *thing*," Lady Tremaine sneered, "is so out of style that it's practically falling to pieces." She reached out a manicured hand to touch Cinderella's sleeve. "Look—the shoulder is frayed." Pulling hard, she ripped the fabric.

"It's falling to bits," she continued, tearing the other side.

Cinderella looked down in shock as Anastasia and Drisella stepped forward, joining their mother on the bottom steps.

"And this! It's hardly sewn on," Drisella said, pulling on a bit of lace at the neckline. "It's a ridiculous, old-fashioned joke!"

Cinderella leaned back, her face filled with horror.

Suddenly, the sound of a carriage interrupted them.

With something new to take their focus, Drisella

and Anastasia turned and headed to peer out the window by the front door.

"Mother!" Anastasia said.

"Look!" Drisella called.

Lady Tremaine looked over her shoulder, then back at Cinderella. "Now cover yourself," she instructed as she turned on her heel. "And when we return from the ball, see that you are dressed decently. People will say we neglect you."

With that, the Tremaines marched out of the house.

And Cinderella was left alone in her tattered dress.

Chapter 13

HE sounds of the Tremaines' carriage clattering away in her ear, Cinderella ran. She didn't know where she was going; she just knew she couldn't stand in the entryway any longer.

She ran through the servants' quarters. She ran out the kitchen door. And then she ran through the garden. Hot tears stung her eyes as she leaned against a wooden fence, her head in her arms. The night's breeze blew against her torn sleeves. She felt like a piece of her had been ripped along with her mother's dress. It was all too much.

"I'm sorry, Mother," she said out loud. "I said I'd believe. I said I'd have courage, but I don't. I don't believe anymore."

"Excuse me, my love. . . ."

"Oh!" Cinderella whipped around at the sound of a

whisper from another. There, sitting against the back of the house, was an old woman she had never seen before. She wore a weathered cloak and held a gnarled wooden walking stick.

"Can you help me, miss?" the woman asked in a trembling voice. "Just a little crust of bread. Or better—a cup of milk?"

Studying the frail, elderly woman, Cinderella felt a pang of shame. How could she be so upset about missing a trivial little ball? She had clothes on her back and food in her stomach, after all. There were so many who had it far worse. She sent a silent thank-you to her mother for the reminder.

Be kind. . . .

Wiping her tears, she straightened her back. "Yes," she said, fixing a soft gaze upon the old woman. "Yes, I think I can find something for you."

Cinderella walked to the table where they kept the pitcher, and filled a wooden bowl with the goat's milk she'd collected that morning.

"You've been crying, my dear," the beggar woman observed.

"It's nothing," Cinderella said, giving her a wistful smile, as she brought the milk over.

The woman bristled. "Nothing? What is a bowl of milk?" she asked, taking the bowl. "Nothing. And everything. Kindness is so rare these days, Ella."

Cinderella started. She wasn't sure if she was more surprised to hear the stranger say her name or to hear it without the word *cinder* in front of it.

The woman set the bowl aside without taking a sip. "Thank you," she said. "Now, I don't mean to hurry you, but we haven't got long, Ella." With that, the woman stood and started walking away.

Cinderella frowned. There was her name again. "How—?"

But the woman was already around the corner. Cinderella rushed to keep up with her.

"How do you know me?" she asked. "Who are you?"

The woman looked around the garden as if searching for something. "Who am I? Well, I should think you'd have worked that out. I'm your fairy godmother, of course."

Cinderella laughed. "But you can't be."

The beggar woman turned to look at her. "Why not?"

Cinderella struggled to find the words. "Because they don't exist. They're just made up for children."

The beggar woman gave her a long, hard look. "Now, you know that's not true. Didn't your own mother tell you she believed in them? And don't say no, because I heard her."

Cinderella was brought back to that moment, right

in that garden, so many years earlier, her mother explaining that fairy godmothers looked after them, just as they looked after the animals.

"I believe in everything," her mother had said.

"You heard her . . . ?" Cinderella asked incredulously.

But the woman now stood a few paces away, staring at a duck that was waddling near the fountain.

"We really ought to get started if you're to make it to the palace in time."

Cinderella frowned, trying to process the impossible thoughts that were running through her head. "In time for what?"

"The ball, child," the woman said, completely exasperated now. "The prince's ball."

Now *that* was something Cinderella could comprehend. Her words came out in a rush. "I can't go to the ball. Look at this dress," she said, gesturing toward the frayed shoulder. "It'll take me days to mend, and it won't be marvelous then. And how would I get there even if I had something to wear? The coach she hired has left—"

"Oh, fiddle-faddle!" the woman said, interrupting her. Then her face lit up, as if she remembered something. "Right. First things first. Let me slip into something more comfortable."

Cinderella watched in bewilderment as the woman lifted her gnarled cane. Suddenly, the beggar woman threw the wooden stick into the air. The seconds it took for the cane to rise and fall back down ticked by slowly as something extraordinary happened:

First a silver glow surrounded the woman. Then the cane shortened and thinned, transforming into a silver wand as it flew through the air. As soon as it pointed down toward the woman, her dark cloak disappeared. And soon Cinderella found herself staring at a beautiful woman with light curls and a sparkling white dress.

"That's better," the Fairy Godmother said, inspecting her new ensemble approvingly.

Cinderella shook her head, utterly amazed. "But how did you—?"

"Now," the woman announced, seeming not to hear Cinderella's question. "Perhaps we should begin with the carriage. To be honest, I hadn't really thought about it, although I can't imagine why not. Let's see."

This is a dream, Cinderella thought. *It must be.* She pinched herself. It stung. *So very strange.*

"What we need is something that sort of says 'coach,'" the Fairy Godmother was saying, interrupting Cinderella's reverie.

The woman started to walk again, surveying the yard.

Cinderella couldn't help getting caught up in the moment, no matter how inexplicable. She followed the woman in the glittering dress.

Then, pointing to an old basin, Cinderella suggested, "That tub?" She wasn't sure if she was humoring the woman or if she truly believed something magical was happening. Either way, she wanted to be of help.

"Doesn't really say 'coach,'" her fairy godmother said.

"The barrel?" Cinderella offered.

"I don't believe so." The woman peered at the wooden barrel to which Cinderella was referring. "I'm thinking fruits and vegetables. Do you grow watermelons?"

Cinderella shook her head. "No."

"A cantaloupe?"

What in the world . . . ? Cinderella smiled. "I don't even know what that is."

The Fairy Godmother seemed to think that over. "Let me see. . . . What about a pumpkin?"

Cinderella's face lit up. *That* she could provide. "We've pumpkins. Here."

She led the blond woman across the yard, and the two entered the fragrant greenhouse. It wasn't quite as well maintained as it had been when her mother had been alive, but Cinderella had harvested all the fruits and vegetables she could. The pumpkins had always grown quite well there. They were the stars of the greenhouse.

The Fairy Godmother bent down, studying the large orange produce. "Splendid!" she said approvingly. "Allow me."

The woman pulled at one of the rounder pumpkins, grimacing from the effort of lifting it off the ground. With a low "humph," she dropped it, and it made a loud *thump*.

"Heavy old thing," the Fairy Godmother said. "Never mind. We'll do it here."

"Do what here?" Cinderella asked.

"Isn't it obvious? Turn the pumpkin into a carriage."

Cinderella stared at the woman. "Oh."

Her fairy godmother raised her wand in the air. Then she looked at Cinderella. "Don't hurry me."

"I won't," Cinderella said.

"I just wish I'd remembered you'd have to get there. . . ." The woman shifted uncomfortably. "You're making me nervous."

"Shall I turn round?" Cinderella asked. Though she could barely believe what she was doing, she thought she might as well make it easier on the poor woman.

"Well, it might be better . . ." the Fairy Godmother started. "Oh, for heaven's sake. Let's just have a go."

The Fairy Godmother pointed her wand at the

pumpkin with a flourish. A cloud of golden stardust burst forth.

And then the pumpkin began to grow. And grow. And grow larger still.

Cinderella looked at the rapidly growing fruit in shock. And then she had a rather concerning thought.

"If it *does* get bigger—"

Suddenly, the pumpkin was as large as the greenhouse. It pushed Cinderella and the Fairy Godmother—who, it was clear, most certainly *did* have magic—against the glass walls.

"Is that what you meant to do?" Cinderella asked, her face smushed between the smooth skin of the pumpkin and the cold glass pane.

"Do you *think* it's what I meant to do?" her fairy godmother replied.

There were only two things that could be done in that moment, really. The first was to laugh. Because how extraordinary, how exhilarating this night was becoming. And the second was to run.

Hand in hand, Cinderella and the magical woman sprinted out the greenhouse door just as the walls shattered. The pumpkin continued to grow, and the glittering glass pieces attached themselves to it, twisting and turning and changing color, until Cinderella was looking at a dazzling golden carriage, the most beautiful and ornate coach she'd ever seen.

"There," the woman said proudly. "An equipage worthy of you."

"You really are my fairy godmother!" Cinderella exclaimed. She didn't know how it was possible, but there it was. Her mother had been right to believe in everything. And how wonderful that her fairy godmother should appear on this of all nights.

"Well, of course," the Fairy Godmother said. "I don't just go about transforming pumpkins for just anybody. Now where are those mice? Ah . . ."

The Fairy Godmother knelt by a bush, parting its leaves to reveal Jacqueline, Gus, Jacob, and Esau. They were trembling, their eyes wide. They seemed just as amazed as Cinderella by what was happening.

"What do you think?" the Fairy Godmother asked them. "Will you help her?"

Tentatively, all four mice poked their noses out of the bush.

"They say yes," the Fairy Godmother said, turning to Cinderella.

"They can talk?" Cinderella asked. She hadn't thought anything else could astonish her that night.

"Oh, certainly," her fairy godmother replied. "And they are very good listeners, too. They have told me all about you."

The Fairy Godmother raised her wand over them, and Cinderella felt a surge of panic. "Don't hurt them, please!" she said, suddenly thinking of the shattered greenhouse.

"I won't hurt them," the Fairy Godmother assured her. "Although, I can't promise not to surprise them."

And with that, the Fairy Godmother made another pass of her wand, instantly transforming the mice into four glossy white horses.

"Oh—they are lovely!" Cinderella cried.

As the horses trotted toward the carriage, Jacqueline paused in front of Cinderella, lowering her head so that Cinderella could pat it.

"Now for the postilions," the Fairy Godmother announced. "Hmmm . . . postilions, postilions. I know! Push that bucket aside."

Cinderella did as she was told, lifting an old bucket nearby. Suddenly, two lizards started to scramble away. The Fairy Godmother waved her wand and a pair of handsome footmen stood before them. They wore garments of sparkling green. Their kind eyes bulged, and one of them flicked his tongue nervously.

"That is very kind of you," Cinderella told the new gentlemen as they took their posts in front of the carriage.

The Fairy Godmother waved her off. "Never mind that. Lizards are restless. Always in need of a change. Now bring me that coachman." She pointed toward the meadow behind the house.

"What coachman?" Cinderella asked.

"Did I say coachman? I meant goose."

Cinderella spotted the goose pecking at some corn. She waved it toward her fairy godmother, who twitched her wand at it. Suddenly, a portly coachman with a long nose appeared in the goose's place. He wore a glittering gold suit that matched the carriage perfectly. His stockings were the orange of his previously webbed feet.

"Now, shoo, shoo, everyone into place." The Fairy Godmother ushered the coachman along. "There's not time to be lost."

As the coachman climbed onto the driver's seat and took the reins, one of the postilions opened the carriage door chivalrously, nodding at Cinderella.

Cinderella stayed where she was, unsure how to proceed. As much as it pained her to admit it, her mother's dress was no longer fit for a ball.

"What now, my dear?" the Fairy Godmother asked. "I don't want to hurry you, but . . ."

"My dress," Cinderella started, lifting the skirt. "I can't go in this dress."

Her fairy godmother looked her up and down. "What's wrong with it?"

"Well, it's in pieces, if you please," Cinderella replied.

"Yes, yes, I remember now," the Fairy Godmother

said vaguely. "Of course, it can be very hard to tell. You see so many fashions when you're a thousand years old."

Cinderella stepped toward the woman who'd already done so much for her. She hated to ask for more, but her stepmother had known what she was doing when she'd torn up the dress: Cinderella wouldn't be let into the ball wearing something so ragged. "Do you think you can mend it?"

"I'll turn it into something new!" the magical woman said happily.

"No, no." Cinderella felt uneasy at the thought. "This was my mother's and I'd like to wear it when I go to the palace. It's almost like taking her with me."

The Fairy Godmother softened. "Very well." She lifted her wand, her eyes twinkling. "But even your late mother won't mind if we gee it up a bit."

Cinderella watched in astonishment as the cloud of stardust descended on her. She started to twirl, laughing as she watched the frayed ends repair themselves and then turn from pale pink to her favorite color: a stunning sky blue. Soft, shimmery fabric seemed to grow on the skirt, creating a full frame.

Looking up, she saw a cloud of fireflies descend and felt them settle around her neck, on her earlobes, and on her hair, which had suddenly styled itself in an elegant half chignon. Pastel-colored butterflies flew all about, landing on the new sweeping neckline. They looked just like the toy butterfly her father had given her.

Cinderella looked down. She could not believe her eyes. She was wearing the most beautiful ball gown she'd ever seen. She smiled gratefully at the Fairy Godmother with tears in her eyes.

"She would have loved it," Cinderella told her fairy godmother. She believed it wholeheartedly; she could just imagine her mother smiling down at her at that very moment. Then, pulling up her skirt, Cinderella started to climb into the carriage.

"Just a moment," the Fairy Godmother said, stopping her. "Are those the best you have?"

Cinderella looked down to see what her fairy godmother was looking at: her worn black slippers. "It's all right," Cinderella said good-naturedly. "No one will see them."

The Fairy Godmother tutted impatiently. "No, no. You really never do know when a little thing like shoes will matter a great deal. Let's have something new for a change. Then you can keep them as a memento."

Her heart swelling in gratitude, Cinderella hurried to take off her shoes and place them by the kitchen door.

When she turned around, her fairy godmother was holding out a sparkling pair of high-heeled shoes.

Cinderella gasped as she took hold of them. "But they're made of glass!"

"You'll be surprised at how comfortable they are," her fairy godmother said as Cinderella slipped them on. The Fairy Godmother was right—they were surprisingly soft and cushioned. They felt as though they were formed to move with her feet.

"Now I really must insist you go, and quickly . . ." Cinderella's fairy godmother was saying. "What is it?"

Cinderella had just had another disheartening thought. "My stepmother and the girls. Won't they have me thrown out if they can?"

"I'll make sure they don't know you," the Fairy Godmother assured her, ushering her into the carriage. "Now you must be off. For you *shall* go to the ball!"

Feeling a rush of excitement, Cinderella settled into the ornate coach. Her fairy godmother stuck her head in the window, suddenly quite serious.

"Oh, Ella! Remember this: the magic will only last so long. With the last echo of the last bell at the last stroke of midnight, the spell will be broken, and all will be as it was before."

Cinderella smiled. "Midnight? That will be more than enough time."

Returning her smile, the Fairy Godmother seemed to relax. "Off you go, then."

"Thank you! Oh, thank you!" Cinderella called, wishing she had something else to give or say to the Fairy Godmother that would fully express her gratitude.

As the carriage clattered off into the night, Cinderella laughed in disbelief. "I *shall* go to the ball!"

THE PRINCE

Chapter 14

THE prince sighed, shifting his weight from one foot to the other. From his spot in the upper balcony of the ballroom, he'd been watching the royal crier announce every guest for the last hour.

Much to his dismay, he was stuck, standing between the Grand Duke and his father, with the Captain nearby. And to his even greater dismay, the one guest he'd hoped would appear was nowhere to be seen.

As his eyes swept over the grand ballroom, which glittered under the glowing chandeliers, he wondered if he'd missed her somehow. He saw the baton-wielding conductor leading the orchestra through a lively waltz. He saw the servants, dressed in tailcoats, walking around with trays topped with hors d'oeuvres and glasses of champagne. He saw the array of guests dressed in their colorful finery milling about.

They'd come from far and wide for this ball, and the excitement was palpable, even from Kit's perch. But all he felt was disappointment that he hadn't seen that kind country girl from the forest.

"Princess Chelina of Zaragosa." Kit turned his attention back to the royal crier and the arriving guests who were descending the grand staircase. "The Duke and Duchess Hawkes of Biggleswade and their daughter, Lady Genevieve d'Houellebecq . . ."

The Grand Duke suddenly exited the balcony, heading to the main floor. Kit shifted, happy to have a bit more room at least.

"Lady Tremaine and her daughters . . ." the royal crier was now saying.

Kit watched as an elegant woman headed down the stairs, waving a fan in front of her face. Her daughters, however, stayed behind, whispering in the royal crier's ear.

The man coughed, then declared, "The very clever Miss Drisella and the very beautiful Miss Anastasia."

Their mother turned on the staircase, gesturing violently for her daughters to come forward. They did, waddling a bit in their satin dresses as they fluttered their own fans about.

Honestly, people took these silly events so seriously. Kit would have laughed out loud if he hadn't been so thoroughly depressed.

"Why do you keep looking at the stairs?" King Frederick asked Kit. "Who are you waiting for?"

The prince looked up. "Oh, no one," he said, sighing.

"It's that girl from the forest, isn't it?" his father said. "That's why you were so . . . ah . . . *generous* with the invitations."

"Father," Kit replied, a twinkle in his eye. "It was for the people."

The king patted his son's hand affectionately. "I know you love the people, Kit, but I also know that your head has been turned."

Kit was about to reply with a witty comeback when he saw his father frown. The king leaned in closer, suddenly serious. "Listen to me, my boy. Never mind where she comes from. I want you to be happy. But you've only met her once in the forest."

"Your Highness." The father and son were interrupted by the Grand Duke. It seemed the pompous fellow had left the balcony to collect one of the guests, for he was leading a dark-haired woman in a lavish ball gown to them. "May I present Princess Chelina of Zaragosa?"

Kit bowed politely.

"You are as handsome as your picture, Your Highness," the princess said. She looked around. "And your little kingdom is enchanting."

This condescending statement was not lost on Kit. "I hope the princess will not find our little kingdom *too* confining."

"It could be bigger with the right friends. And enough soldiers," she said, stepping closer. She shot him a broad smile that displayed all of her teeth like a tiger on the prowl.

The prince was taken aback by her forwardness. "I'm not sure I understand."

"Of course you do," Princess Chelina replied, giving him a knowing look. "They tell me you are very brave in battle."

Kit did not know how to respond to this smiling statement of worldly ambition. He frowned but was suddenly distracted by a small commotion that was taking place below.

The music had stopped, and a chorus of murmurs sounded in its place. "Who is that?" "Where did she come from?" Most of the guests were staring at the grand staircase. Kit followed their gazes . . .

. . . and there she was.

A vision in periwinkle gliding down the staircase. Though every eye was now on her, and the whispers clearly about her, she seemed the very definition of composure. She smiled confidently, her step as graceful as a swan in water.

It was the girl from the forest—it had to be! True, she was dressed more formally now, her neck and ears adorned with sparkling jewels. But that beautiful face, those kind, warm eyes, that poise and self-assurance . . . Kit would have recognized her anywhere.

She must be a princess, Kit realized suddenly. That could be the only explanation; she wore the finest gown in the room, and her demeanor was the easy regality many of the other guests had attempted and failed to achieve.

Perhaps she hadn't wanted to fluster a simple apprentice by revealing her true identity. Kit let out a chortle of incredulity. To think they had more in common than he'd thought, each hiding their nobility from the other.

Kit suddenly noticed that the princess Chelina was staring at him, hers the only pair of eyes in the room that were not on the staircase, Kit would have wagered.

"Excuse me," he said, moving past the Grand Duke to get to the staircase.

"A thousand apologies, Princess," he heard the Duke clamor as he left. "I don't know what happened."

His father's kind voice came next: "He's a bit of a dreamer. Like his father."

Kit made it to the main floor and then stopped cold. She'd seen him. Their eyes met and Kit's heart began to beat out of his chest; his palms started sweating.

As they walked toward each other, it seemed as though time stood still. The guests parted like waves and moved to the various sides of the room. Finally, Kit and the mystery woman met in the middle of the empty dance floor.

"Mr. Kit . . ." she said softly.

"It's you . . . isn't it?" the prince asked, unsure what else to say.

She smiled. "Just so."

Kit took a deep breath. "If I may—that is . . . it would give me the greatest pleasure if you would do me the honor of letting me lead you through the . . . the next . . ."

He paused. *Oh God, what is it called?* What was he trying to ask her?

"Dance?" the woman supplied.

The prince grinned sheepishly. "Yes, dance. That's it."

The woman nodded demurely, and he held out his hand. As she took it, they both gasped, staring at each other. *Did she feel that, too?* Kit wondered. *That spark?*

Just then, as though they'd suddenly realized they were needed, the orchestra started playing their instruments, and beautiful music soared through the ballroom.

"They are all looking at you," the woman said, leaning in.

"Believe me," Kit said, laughing, "they are all looking at *you*."

And with that, they were off, caught up in the dance. They moved together easily, not taking their eyes off each other. Kit led her across the ballroom in a traditional waltz.

He felt her lean into increasingly advanced twists and turns, which they performed perfectly, all the while keeping in perfect time. It was like they had danced every dance together, like they had been dancing partners their entire lives.

His hands were shaking and he was sure that his palms were moist. But the woman didn't seem to notice. She just looked at him with those bright, intelligent eyes of hers. She seemed to be looking at him with a curious fascination, which made Kit feel both nervous and thrilled simultaneously.

As the music swelled to its finishing crescendo, they spun. Kit lifted the woman, then dipped her gracefully just as the song ended. There was a moment of hushed amazement before the guests burst into applause.

Kit could see the woman looking around at the audience they had procured. She seemed surprised to see that so many people had stopped to watch them. Just as Kit was going to ask her if she was all right, a lady in chartreuse rushed up to them. "Your Highness," she started, curtseying.

He saw shock register across the mystery girl's face. " 'Your Highness'?" she repeated.

Oh no. They couldn't have this conversation in front of all these people. Making a split-second decision, the prince took her hand.

"Come with me," he said, leading her across the dance floor and out a side door.

It was time to explain. He just hoped she wouldn't be too upset with him.

CINDERELLA

Chapter 15

INDERELLA couldn't believe it. Mr. Kit—the sweet, somewhat anxious apprentice she'd met in the forest—was actually not an apprentice at all.

They walked along a quiet, dimly lit gallery. Paintings of all sorts of royalty and nobility lined the walls.

"So you are the *prince*," Cinderella finally said, not hiding the incredulity in her voice.

"Well, not *the* prince, exactly," the man answered. He chuckled nervously. "There are plenty of other princes in the world. I'm only *a* prince."

Cinderella frowned, turning her head to look at him. "Then your name is not really Kit?"

"Oh, certainly it is," the prince assured her. "My father still calls me that, when he is especially unannoyed at me."

"I see. But you are no apprentice."

Kit shook his head. "I am! I'm an apprentice *monarch*. Still learning my trade."

Cinderella stared at him and he sighed. "Please forgive me. I thought you might treat me differently if you knew. I mistook *you* for a simple country girl. But now I see that you didn't want to overawe a plain soldier."

Feeling a blush creep over her, Cinderella smiled. "Little chance of that," she said. She could not fault him for trying to hide his identity. Hadn't she avoided telling him her name for the very same reason?

They stopped their walk, and Kit held out his hand. "No more surprises?" he asked.

Cinderella paused for just a second before shaking it. "No more surprises." She would tell him her name and story eventually. For now, she just wanted to enjoy the night.

Looking up, she saw a familiar face in a portrait of a young man on horseback. "Is that you?" she asked.

Kit nodded, reddening. "I hate myself in paintings. Don't you?"

Cinderella laughed. "No one has ever painted my portrait."

"No? They should."

Cinderella smiled, unsure of how to reply. She peered back up at Kit's portrait, studying it. "What were you doing?"

"That? Oh . . . I was about to charge the enemy," Kit explained.

"How terrible," Cinderella said without thinking.

The prince cocked his head at her. "Most people would say, 'How exciting.'"

"I'm sorry," Cinderella said. She was afraid she'd offended him.

"Don't be," Kit replied. He looked at her with surprise. "You're right. It is terrible. I'm not supposed to say that . . . but it is. . . ."

Suddenly, Cinderella remembered the conversation she'd overheard at her stepmother's last dinner party.

"And the prince so young and callow. They say he has no stomach for fighting. . . ."

"But he is a dreamy fellow all the same, believes in the rights of man and universal peace. All that sort of nonsense."

She looked at Kit, a newfound respect in her eyes. Maybe they had more in common than she had thought.

Cinderella and Kit spent the next couple of hours wandering around the palace, talking, exchanging childhood stories. They meandered through the expansive gardens under the light of the full moon.

"Here is where I played when I was little," the prince said, pointing to a patch of grass between perfectly rectangular hedges.

Cinderella smiled at the thought. "And who did you play with?"

"The Captain of the Guard, kind fellow that he is," Kit said. "And you? Who did you have to play with?"

"Oh, I had so many playmates—sheep, and geese, and all the mice, of course."

Kit searched her eyes, seeming to try to figure out if she was teasing him. "Of course. Are they good company?"

Cinderella nodded, thinking of all her animal friends had done for her that night, and all her life, really. "They are excellent listeners."

Spotting an ornate Grecian fountain, Cinderella gasped. "How beautiful!"

"My mother loved it here," Kit said wistfully. "Since she died, my father can't bring himself to visit the gardens."

Cinderella looked at him. "My mother is in heaven, too." She hoped to alleviate some of the pain in his eyes. "Do you suppose they know each other?"

Kit grinned. "I don't see why not."

"Exactly," Cinderella said, walking forward. "I think heaven is like the palace ball. Everyone is invited."

"That's because of you," Kit said. Cinderella turned

to look at him questioningly. "I made sure that every-one could come . . . because I hoped to see you again."

Cinderella couldn't help feeling a rush of joy at this notion. "And I came to see Mr. Kit," she admitted.

"Not the prince?" Kit asked.

"Oh, no," Cinderella said, a twinkle in her eye. "The prince is far too grand."

Kit laughed merrily. "Surely not for someone like you."

They looked at each other. Then Kit spoke once more. "I don't suppose you have a large army?"

Cinderella blinked at the non sequitur. "I'm afraid I have no army at all."

"Pity," the prince said. "The Grand Duke would have liked that."

They made their way to a tree-lined path, which glowed under the light of amber torches.

"Won't they miss you at the ball?" Cinderella asked.

"Maybe," the prince said. "But let's not go back just yet."

Cinderella noticed a slight edge to his voice. "What's wrong?" she asked.

Kit sighed. "When I go back, they will try to pair me off with a lady of their choosing. I am expected to marry for advantage."

Cinderella was taken aback. "Oh. Whose advantage?"

Looking up at her, Kit grinned. "That's a good question."

Cinderella couldn't imagine having to marry a person of someone else's choosing. True, her living conditions were not favorable. But at least she wasn't *forced* into them. And at least she had control of whom she loved. Kit, on the other hand . . . "Surely you have a right to your own heart?"

"I must weigh that against the king's wishes," Kit explained. "He is a wise ruler and a loving father."

"Perhaps he will change his mind," Cinderella offered.

Kit looked down, his voice suddenly filled with emotion. "I fear he hasn't much time to do so."

The gravity of the situation dawned on Cinderella. She felt sympathy—no, *empathy*—for what Kit was experiencing. He seemed close to his parents, just as she had been to hers. And soon, it seemed, he would be an orphan, like her.

She reached out and gently touched his arm. "You are a good son."

Kit looked at her with gratitude. "Perhaps." Then an idea lit up his eyes. "Would you like to see my very favorite place?"

Cinderella smiled and nodded.

It turned out Kit's favorite place was another garden, though this one was much different from the others. It was accessed through a secret wooden door off an enclosed path covered in vines. It was enchantingly lush and overgrown, as though everyone else had forgotten it existed.

"A secret garden!" Cinderella cried, delighted.

The prince ran ahead and took hold of a majestic old wooden swing tied to a tree, its ropes intertwined with flowers. He offered the seat to Cinderella.

"I shouldn't," Cinderella said.

"You should," he responded.

"Yes, I should," Cinderella said, grinning. She gently lowered herself onto the swing. Behind her, Kit placed his hands on the small of her back, and Cinderella gasped at the touch.

"May I?" he asked.

Her heart started to beat quicker. "Please," she allowed. And with that, he pushed her lightly. The swing creaked as she swung back and forth.

The evening breeze tickled her face, and she breathed in the scent of jasmine, the night-blooming flower, all around them. It felt as though they were in a fairyland.

Suddenly, one of Cinderella's glass slippers flew off her foot and fell some distance away on the grass.

"Oh!" she cried.

The prince ran to collect the slipper as Cinderella slowed the swing. He walked back toward her, gazing in wonder at the sparkling slipper in hand.

"It's made of glass," he said.

Cinderella laughed. What a strange and completely wonderful night. "And why not?"

The prince knelt down in front of her and slid the slipper back onto her foot. He looked up at her.

"There," he said quietly.

"There," Cinderella repeated softly.

"Won't you tell me who you really are?" Kit asked, standing.

Cinderella felt a surge of nervousness as she rose from the swing. This was it. The moment of honesty. And yet—"If I do . . . I think everything might be . . . different."

"I don't understand," the prince said. "Can you at least tell me your name?"

Have courage. Be kind. "My name . . ." Cinderella started. She took a deep breath, ready. "My name is—"

Suddenly, she noticed the gigantic palace clock tower, visible behind Kit. She felt herself become still at a sudden realization.

It was almost midnight.

Chapter 16

INDERELLA stared at the face of the glowing clock just about to ring the hour. In no time, she would be back in her tattered rags. The animals would be scrambling around the front of the palace next to a large pumpkin parked in the drive.

"I have to leave!" she cried. "It's hard to explain . . . lizards, pumpkins . . ." After taking one last look at the prince, who had a very sweet yet very confused expression on his face, she bolted to the hidden door to the vine-covered passage.

"Wait!" she heard him call after her. "Where are you going?"

Ohhhh. She couldn't just leave without another word. She stuck her head through an opening in the vines to look back at him.

"You've been awfully nice. Thank you for a

wonderful evening! I loved it—every second!" she cried.

And then Cinderella ran faster than she'd ever run in her entire life. She ran down the covered path. She ran through the ornamental gardens, past the rows of hedges. She ran across the palace terrace and then in through the gallery, past Kit's portrait.

Flinging the side door open, Cinderella ran back into the ballroom, where half the guests were engaged in a mad polka. Cinderella ducked and dove between the dancers, heading away from the dance floor.

Just then, she found herself bumping into Anastasia and Drisella, knocking the dainties they were about to eat out of their hands.

"Sorry!" she called.

"It was nothing, Your Highness!" she heard Drisella say.

Cinderella's eyes widened, but there was no time to marvel. As she continued to flee, lapdogs were sent scampering, glasses dropped to the ground, shrieks of surprise were uttered.

Cinderella turned her head to make sure she hadn't done any more damage when—

SMACK!

She looked up and saw that she'd collided with King Frederick himself.

"Oh! Your Highness!" she cried. "I'm—I'm so sorry."

The king smiled at her. "Think nothing of it, my dear."

Cinderella turned to go. Then, suddenly, she paused, looking back at the king. When else would she have this chance?

"I just wanted to say, Your Highness," Cinderella started, "your son, Kit, is the most lovely person I ever met. So good and brave. I hope you know how much he loves you."

Her sentiments shared, she sprinted off, not waiting to see the king's reaction.

Cinderella dashed through the courtyard, flanked with guards. She could see the golden carriage gleaming at the bottom of the staircase, the two elegantly garbed footmen standing in front of it.

Almost there, she thought.

Cinderella lifted her gown and dashed down the steps two at a time. Suddenly, she tripped, feeling the slipper that had flown off on the swing earlier slide off her foot once more.

Turning, Cinderella saw that the guards had appeared at the top of the stairs. And another figure was there, too, calling after her. Was that Kit? There was no time to find out. She'd have to leave the slipper behind. Taking off the other shoe and clutching it against her chest, Cinderella ran barefoot the rest of the way.

She made it to the carriage, and the former lizard helped her up the steps and inside. With a loud "Ya!" that sounded remarkably like a honk, the coachman set the horses off. The carriage clamored into the night.

"Come on, goosey," Cinderella called out the window, the wind blowing in her hair.

BONG . . . BONG . . . The clock tower rang.

Was that the fourth bell? The sixth? Cinderella did not know. She turned to look at the clock and found that her carriage was being pursued by a fleet of horses.

The coachman's nose suddenly became a beak, while the footmen grew tails. Thinking quickly, one of them used his new appendage to close the palace gates behind them, buying them a bit more time.

"Well done," Cinderella called to the rapidly transforming footman.

Inside the carriage, the walls were starting to turn a bright orange. The ride was getting bumpier by the second.

"You can do it, goosey," Cinderella yelled to the coachman encouragingly.

BONG . . .

They clattered through the town square and across

a bridge. The loud clacking of hoofbeats echoed in Cinderella's ears.

BONG...

Turning to see if the horsemen had caught up, Cinderella suddenly found the carriage's now slimy walls closing in on her.

"Ahhh!" Cinderella felt her head, arms, and feet push through the gourd-like walls, as though she were dressing in a giant pumpkin. Using the momentum they'd built, she ran, acting as the former carriage's wheels. The horses in front of her were starting to transform back into mice, their ears rounding, their whiskers sprouting, their bodies shrinking. Then their reins disappeared altogether.

BONG... BONG...

Cinderella slowed to a stop just as the pumpkin cracked and fell off her. They were just off the road, in a small grove by a lake. The mice scurried by her side, and the two lizards darted nearby. A few paces away, the goose waddled, flapping its wings, and then flew off into the night.

Cinderella looked down and saw that her grand ball gown had turned back into the pink tattered dress. To her surprise, the remaining glass slipper was still in her hand, with not a scratch on it.

She heard hoofbeats approaching. Thinking quickly, she held the slipper behind her back as a man on horseback rode up to her. She recognized him as the scowling gentleman who'd been standing next to Kit when she'd arrived at the ball. *The Grand Duke,* she thought.

"Identify yourself," the Duke barked from his saddle.

"They call me Cinderella," she answered.

The Grand Duke glared down at her. "Cinderella? What sort of name is that? Who are you?"

Cinderella shook her head. No good would come from talking to this man; she could see that quite plainly. "Me? I am no one."

"You certainly don't look like anyone," he replied, giving her the once-over. "And yet . . . that dress looks familiar. Were you at the ball?"

Cinderella looked down at her tattered dress. "Who would wear these rags to the ball, sir?"

The Duke nodded, though he still seemed suspicious. "There was a carriage on the road with a princess inside. Think carefully—the future of the kingdom is at risk."

Cinderella was taken aback. What did he mean by that? Why on earth would the future of the kingdom be at risk? Did he think she was part of some grand plot that threatened the throne?

"I don't know any princesses, my lord," she answered truthfully.

"No, how could you?" the Duke said. "Yet . . . there is something about you. . . ." He peered down, taking a closer look at her.

Cinderella stared back at him evenly.

Suddenly, they were interrupted by the clopping of more horses. The Captain of the Guard appeared, leading several other guards.

He looked at her, puzzled, perhaps on the brink of recognition. He had, after all, been in the forest with Kit the day they had met.

"Captain, escort this girl home," the Duke ordered.

"Mademoiselle." The Captain bowed his head.

"That's not necessary," Cinderella said, quickly turning around. She needed to leave the grove before the Captain placed her face. Who knew what the Duke would do with a servant girl masquerading as a princess, however inadvertent it had been? "I know the way."

Heading down the road, she let out her breath only when she heard the hooves of the horses start off in the other direction. That had been close.

Just then, Cinderella felt tiny feet scurry next to her. "Oh!" she cried, bending down toward the four mice. "I'm sorry. In you get." She lowered the glass slipper so that they could climb in. They would still ride in elegance the rest of the way home.

It started to rain. Ella covered the slipper holding the mice with one hand and then laughed, feeling the cool water run over her. She shook her wet hair. What a night it had been. A night to remember forever.

"The prince was showing me a great deal of favor," Anastasia told Cinderella, taking a biscuit from the tray Cinderella held in front of her.

"I thought his eye was more inclined towards me," Drisella said.

Though it was quite late, the Tremaines had insisted on taking tea in the parlor as soon as they had returned, gushing about the evening's events. They'd barely blinked an eye when they'd seen Cinderella in her wet, tattered dress, immediately accepting her tale of taking a stroll in the rain to cheer herself up. They were too caught up in reliving the ball to pay much attention to their disheveled stepsister.

For her part, Cinderella was having a hard time keeping a straight face at her stepsisters' embellishments. She couldn't help encouraging them a bit.

"What did he say to you?" she asked innocently.

Anastasia and Drisella exchanged looks.

"What do you mean, what did he *say*?" Anastasia asked.

Drisella sniffed. "Don't be so common, Cinderella.

We did not communicate with mere *words*. Our *souls* met."

Cinderella had to turn around at this, pretending to fix the tea things.

"Precisely," Anastasia replied to her sister. "My soul and the prince's soul. *Your* soul was over by the banquet tables."

"You didn't *speak* to him, let alone *dance!*" Lady Tremaine snapped. She'd been very quiet up till then, silently stewing in her seat at the table.

"It was not our fault, Mother," Anastasia whined. "It was that girl—"

"The mystery princess!" Drisella added.

Cinderella turned around. "*Mystery princess*? My, what a charming notion."

"There was no princess," her stepmother said slowly. "It was a preening interloper who made a spectacle of herself."

"Oh?" Cinderella said. Her mind's eye had transported her back to the ball, searching the sea of faces from the grand staircase before landing on Kit's.

"A vulgar young hussy marched into the ball, unaccompanied, if you will, and threw herself at the prince," Lady Tremaine was saying.

Anastasia took a sip of her tea. "And he actually danced with the ugly thing."

Danced. Cinderella sighed as the lively waltz floated into her head. She swayed a bit, imagining Kit's hand on hers, their movements perfectly aligned as they glided across the dance floor. "Yes?" she said dreamily.

"Yes!" Drisella repeated. "It was *pity*. He was too polite to send her packing in front of everyone, you see. But not wanting to expose us to the presumptuous wench any further, he took her apart—"

"And told her off!" Anastasia finished. "But she refused to leave, and the palace guard chased her from the party!"

Her reverie broken by this ridiculous notion, Cinderella turned away from her stepsisters once more, trying hard to keep from smiling.

"I pity the prince," Anastasia continued. "Such bad taste."

"They belong together," Drisella agreed.

Lady Tremaine stood, looking at Cinderella pointedly. "It's no matter. The ball was mere diversion. He's promised to the princess Chelina of Zaragosa. The Grand Duke told me as much himself."

Cinderella froze. Kit had said he was expected to marry for advantage. But he was already betrothed?

"It's so very unfair," Drisella remarked.

"I suppose it wasn't meant to be," Lady Tremaine said.

But Cinderella barely heard them. Quietly excusing herself, she left the room in a daze.

What had she expected? No matter how she'd felt

around him, she'd met him on only two occasions. And he was a prince. It was not like they would be able to continue to meet.

She climbed the steps of the attic, resolved to keep her chin up and not cry. She should be grateful for the time they'd spent together, grateful for that *borrowed* time. She should hope that poor Kit would grow to love his betrothed. For not having the freedom to marry whom one loved—that was a fate worse than anything.

Cinderella entered the dark attic, headed to the loose floorboard that held her treasures, and lifted it. She took the glass slipper out of her apron pocket and held it close to her face. It sparkled under the moonlight glowing from the window.

Smiling wistfully, Cinderella placed the shoe next to her toy butterfly and her mother's portrait. That was what the night would be for her—another perfect memory.

Suddenly, she heard squeaking behind her. She turned to see Jacqueline, Gus, Jacob, and Esau peeking up at her.

"Thank you for your help," she told them, petting each soft head with her finger. "It was like a dream. Better than a dream."

THE PRINCE

Chapter 17

KIT stormed into the Grand Duke's apartment. Though he knew it wasn't the Duke's fault that the woman had fled the ball without leaving so much as her name, he couldn't help taking out his frustration on the man. Especially since the Duke insisted he focus his energies elsewhere, namely on marrying someone else. And besides, it didn't seem like the Duke was trying very hard to find the mystery girl, despite his orders.

"Is there any news?" the prince asked, striding up to the Duke's mahogany desk.

The Duke rose. "None, Your Highness."

Kit turned and started pacing about the room, his head down. "It can't be. Someone like that doesn't just vanish."

What had he not thought of? Why had she gone? Was she in some sort of trouble? She seemed as though she'd liked him, had enjoyed spending time with him. Was he imagining that his feelings for her had been requited to make himself feel better? Kit felt a flicker of uneasiness at the thought.

"She appeared from nowhere," the Grand Duke countered. "Why should she not return to nowhere? Do you not find it just a little suspect?"

The prince looked up at the Duke. "What?"

Walking around from behind his desk, the Duke spoke firmly. "The sudden arrival of a mysterious stranger. Her uncanny affinity for Your Highness." He paused, letting this insinuation sink in. "I have no doubt that this was a carefully conceived plot."

"To what end?"

"To weaken the kingdom by foiling a marriage arrangement with the princess Chelina. This 'mystery princess' was the agent of a foreign power!"

Kit nearly laughed. The woman he'd danced with, talked with, shared with . . . a spy? Someone plotting to take down the kingdom? It was ridiculous. He hadn't imagined her sincerity, her genuine goodness; he knew that much with certainty.

"You're deluded," the prince told the man.

But the Grand Duke was not deterred. "Am I? Where

is she? What was the meaning of last night's charade?"

"She was no schemer." The prince was starting to get angry. "She is good, and kind, and wise—"

"And missing," the Duke supplied evenly.

The next two weeks were filled with more heartache for Kit. His father's condition suddenly took a turn for the worse, postponing all missions to find the mystery girl. Kit spent as much time at his father's bedside as he could, reading to him, reminiscing about happier times, or simply sitting with him quietly.

One evening, Kit was taking a late dinner, when he was summoned by a servant.

"Your Highness, come quick. To your father's chambers!"

Kit ran the halls and hurried into the airy round chamber. The royal physician was packing up his tools. He exchanged sad looks with Kit, bowed his head, and then exited.

Kit felt his heart sink as he approached the four-poster bed that held his frail father.

"You've come," King Frederick said when he spotted Kit. "Good."

"Father, what's happened?" Kit asked, reaching out to hold the man's hand.

"What happens to us all in time, my boy," his father said wistfully.

Kit shook his head, sinking into the chair next to his father's bed. "Not to you. Not to my king. Not to my father. You will recover."

The king chuckled. "You must learn to lie better than that if you will be a good statesman."

Kit laughed with him, tears springing into his eyes. He realized these moments of playful banter with his father, these wonderful moments, were numbered. "Father, don't go."

"I must," the king said, squeezing his son's hand. "But you needn't be alone. Take a bride." He searched his son's eyes. "What if I commanded you to do so?"

Kit sighed. He didn't want to upset his father, especially at this of all times. But he couldn't make a false promise. "I know that you want me to marry for advantage."

"And?" King Frederick prompted gently.

"And I will not. I'm sorry. I love and respect you, but I won't." Kit hurried on. He'd thought about this a lot in the past couple of weeks. "I believe we need not look outside our borders for strength or guidance.

What we need is right before us. We need only . . . have courage and be kind to see it."

The king looked at his son, tears welling in his eyes now, too. "Just so," he said softly. "You have become your own man. Good. And perhaps, in the little time left to me, I can become the father you deserve."

Kit shook his head, surprised. He began to protest. His father had been wonderful. But the king was not finished.

"You must not marry for advantage," his father continued. "You must marry for love. Find that *girl* they are talking about." He had a twinkle in his eye. "The forgetful one . . ."

"Who loses her shoes," Kit joined in, laughing again. He sighed, deeply touched by his father's approval of the mystery girl. Then he grew serious. "But the Grand Duke—"

"Will never rule so long as you are not mastered by him," the king finished. Squeezing his son's hand again, he smiled. "Be cheerful, my boy. Have courage, and be kind."

Kit was moved to hear those familiar words repeated to him. "I love you, Father."

"I love you, Son."

Kit crawled onto the bed beside his father, his best

friend, his king, letting the tears fall freely. It was a moment pure and honest, the most he could have hoped for in such awful circumstances. He would never forget it, not for the rest of his days.

INDERELLA

Chapter 18

 month passed as the kingdom mourned the loss of its king. Cinderella mourned for Kit, hoping he was faring okay after the loss of his father. She wanted to go to him, to comfort him. But she knew that even if she could get as far as the palace, there would be no way the guards would let a girl dressed as a servant see the ew king. And a small part of her wondered if he would even want to see her after she'd left the way she had, after weeks without contact.

So Cinderella went on with life in the way she had before the ball. She worked hard to care for the house and all the animals who resided in and outside of it. She kept her parents' memories alive, thinking of them as she tended to the garden or when a quote came to mind. She catered to the Tremaines' whims and desires, treating them kindly, as she would want to be treated, replaying the night of the ball in her head or taking Galahad out for a ride whenever she was in need of a break.

She still loved the days when she could ride Galahad to town. She would visit with Flora and the other former servants who lived nearby and chat with the shopkeepers. Cinderella enjoyed seeing what new foods and products they had to offer, the fresh fish set out by the monger, the new colors of fabric the seamstress had.

Unfortunately, Anastasia and Drisella had recently taken a liking to going to town, as well. Cinderella suspected they'd grown weary of staying cooped up in the house all day and tormenting each other. So whenever they saw her preparing the saddle for Galahad, they insisted that she hitch up her father's old cart so that they could go along.

"Oh, very pretty!" Drisella preened, examining a large colorful hat that was on display in one of the vendor's stalls.

"I want it," Anastasia said, bumping into her sister. "It would look so much better on *me*."

Cinderella sighed. She often had to treat her stepsisters like children, reminding them that they could not afford to buy anything superfluous. Though this often did not deter them.

"Hear ye! Hear ye!"

They were interrupted by the fanfare and booming voice of the royal crier. He was standing on the platform in the middle of the square, holding a large scroll. A crowd gathered in front of him.

Immediately recalling the last time she'd heard a proclamation in the square—a proclamation that had changed her life, at least for one night—Cinderella walked closer to the scene. People bustled around her. Clearly, she was not the only one eager to hear the news from the palace.

The crier began his announcement: "Know that our new king hereby declares his love for the mysterious princess who wore glass slippers to the ball, and requests she present herself at the palace, whereupon, if she be willing, he will forthwith marry her, with all due ceremony."

Cinderella felt her heart leap out of her chest. Kit! He wanted to see her . . . he wanted to marry her. She could hardly believe it. He felt the way about her that she felt about him. He was refusing to marry the princess Chelina, choosing her instead.

She shook her head, trying to clear her thoughts.

"How grotesque." Cinderella turned to see that Anastasia and Drisella were right beside her, holding identical frilly hatboxes.

"He's making a fool of himself," Anastasia added.

Ignoring them, Cinderella repeated the crier's

words in her head: *"The mysterious princess who wore glass slippers . . ."*

That was it! She might look like nothing more than a servant girl, but she had one of the glass slippers. All she had to do was bring that to the palace and her identity would be verified.

Cinderella ran toward Galahad, leaving Anastasia and Drisella behind. She had to get home right away to collect the slipper. She had wasted enough time. Soon she would be with Kit.

Besides, her stepsisters would find their way back.

Exhausted and breathless, Cinderella flung open the attic door. She rushed to her secret hiding space, the only place that was truly and completely *hers*, the loose floorboard. Hastily lifting it, she found—

—the frame of her mother's portrait was cracked. The toy butterfly had had its wings ripped off. And there was no sign of the glass slipper.

"Are you looking for this?"

Startled, Cinderella looked up to see her step-mother at the other end of the room, wading in the shadows. She wore a cold look on her face. And in her hand, she held Cinderella's slipper.

"There must be quite a story to go with it," Lady Tremaine posited. "Will you tell me?"

Cinderella stared at her, shock and anger welling up inside.

"No?" Lady Tremaine said. "Then I will tell you a story." She paused, setting her steely gaze on Cinderella before beginning her tale. "There was a beautiful young girl who married for love. She had two loving daughters. All was well. But then her husband, the light of her life, died."

Cinderella's stepmother leaned forward, her face half cast in shadow. "The next time she married for the sake of her children. But this man, too, was taken from her." She smiled. "And I was doomed to look every day upon his beloved child."

Cinderella shifted, keeping her eyes on her stepmother.

"I had hoped to marry off one of my beautiful, stupid daughters to the prince," Lady Tremaine continued. "But his head was turned by a girl with glass slippers. And so I lived unhappily ever after." She looked down, examining the sparkling shoe in her hands. "My story would appear to be ended. Now, tell me yours. Did you steal it?"

Cinderella shook her head. "It was given to me."

"Given to you," Lady Tremaine repeated, laughing. "Nothing is ever *given*. For everything, we must pay."

"That's not true," Cinderella said, taking a step toward her. "Kindness is free. Love is free."

"You're wrong. Love costs us everything," Lady Tremaine countered, her voice filled with emotion.

Then, seeming to calm herself, she dangled the slipper from her finger. Cinderella watched in horror as it swayed, perilously close to falling on the hard floor.

"Now, here is how *you* will pay *me* if you are to have what you desire," Lady Tremaine said, walking forward. "No one will believe you, a dirty servant girl without family, if you make a claim to the prince's heart. But with a respectable gentlewoman putting you forward . . ." She stopped and touched her hand to her chest. Then she resumed her stride, walking past Cinderella to the other side of the room.

"You will not be ignored. When you are married, you will make me the head of the royal household. Anastasia and Drisella, we will pair off with wealthy lords. And I will manage the boy."

"He's not a boy," Cinderella interjected.

"Oh?" Her stepmother grinned. "And who are you? How would *you* rule a kingdom?" she asked condescendingly. "Best to leave it to me. This way we all get what we want."

"No," Cinderella answered immediately.

"No?"

Cinderella could not believe this was happening, could not believe the threats her stepmother was making. But she would not let it go any further.

"I will not allow you to ruin the palace the way you ruined my home. I was not able to protect my father from you . . . but I *will* protect the prince and the kingdom. No matter what becomes of me."

Lady Tremaine stared at her opponent, the anger clear in her tight mouth and shaking hands. "So—you are courageous to boot. That is a mistake."

Suddenly, impulsively, Lady Tremaine smashed the slipper against the wall. It broke with a heart-wrenching *crack* and left the stepmother holding one large, sharp glass shard.

"Stop!" Cinderella cried. It was too much. It had finally been too much. "*Why?* Why are you so cruel? I don't understand it. I have tried to be kind."

"You—kind to *me*?" Lady Tremaine repeated, aghast.

"Yes!" Cinderella replied emphatically. She could not stop now. Enough was enough. "Though you do not deserve it. And though no one deserves to be treated as you have treated me." And then she repeated the question she'd wondered for a very long time. "Why do you do it? *Why?*"

Lady Tremaine looked as though she'd been deflated. She squinted, seeming to search for words.

"Why? Why? Because you are young, and innocent, and good, and I . . . I am *not*."

With that, Lady Tremaine opened the door and exited, slamming it. Cinderella heard the horrifying sound of the lock clicking as she ran toward it.

She pushed and pushed against the door, then pounded on it, yelling for somebody to let her out. It was no use.

Cinderella was trapped.

INTERLUDE

Chapter 19

I had been a long day for the Grand Duke. First that nonsense with the prince—*king* now—insisting on that ridiculous proclamation about the mystery girl. And now he was receiving random visits from nobodies in the kingdom. True, this was a very beautiful nobody. But still, these were not the types of duties a grand duke should be dealing with.

The woman—Lady Tremaine, she'd said her name was—sat in front of him, a small smile on her lips. She seemed quite comfortable. She didn't speak for a few moments, just staring at him. Then, quite suddenly, she pulled a shard of sparkling glass out of her bag and set it on the table between them.

The Duke stiffened. There was no doubt about it. This could only have come from the glass slipper that matched the one currently in the king's possession. It had the same light, airy texture, the same remarkable shimmer that seemed to display all the colors in the world at once.

"May I ask where you got this?" he said slowly.

"From a ragged servant girl in my household," Lady Tremaine answered.

The Duke shook his head, trying to make sense of it all. "Then the 'mystery princess' is a commoner."

"You can imagine—when I discovered her subterfuge—how horrified I was," the woman said.

Hundreds of thoughts raced through the Grand Duke's mind. He had promised months earlier that the young king would marry Princess Chelina. Of course, he'd arranged to have more time after King Frederick's death, but he knew the kingdom of Zaragosa wouldn't wait around forever. Kit could absolutely not hear about this servant girl.

"And you came straight to me?" he asked, praying she would say yes.

Lady Tremaine lowered her head, smiling more broadly now. "Of course. I have heard that you are the most honorable man in the kingdom."

The Duke returned her smile, admiring her pluck. "You told no one else," he said.

"Not even my own daughters," Lady Tremaine replied, placing a hand to her heart.

The Duke allowed himself a sigh of relief. "And the girl . . ."

"Is in a safe place," the woman finished.

The Duke nodded. "You have spared the kingdom from a great deal of embarrassment."

"And I hope to keep it that way," Lady Tremaine said without skipping a beat.

Aha. So there was the other shoe dropping. "Are you threatening me?"

The smile remained on Lady Tremaine's face. "Yes."

Raising his eyebrows, the Grand Duke sat up straighter. At least she was honest about her intentions. He couldn't say the same for most of the dignitaries he dealt with on a regular basis. "I see. Thank you for being plain. What do you want?"

"A title for myself and advantageous marriages for my two daughters."

That was not bad, considering all she could have asked for with such information. "Done," he agreed. "And the girl?"

Lady Tremaine shrugged. "Do with her what you will. She's nothing to me."

"If you play me false, good lady . . ." The Grand Duke stopped, seeing in her stoic face that Lady Tremaine meant what she said. She did not seem to have any attachment to the girl whatsoever. He smiled at the poised woman, continuing.

"Well. The young king will take some convincing. He is . . . willful. But keep this girl out of sight until we may profitably marry him off, and you will get what you desire."

THE KING

Chapter 20

KIT paced the throne room. He knew he had other matters to think about, other *kingly* matters. There were diplomats to meet, treaties to look over. But he could not focus.

The proclamation had gone out only a day earlier, but still, he was anxious. He had thought—no, he had *hoped*—that the girl would have come forward by then. The Captain of the Guard stood nearby, looking concerned.

Suddenly, the Grand Duke strode in, his shoes clacking on the floor. He held something in his hand. Only when the Duke held it up to Kit's face did Kit realize what it was.

It was a shard of glass. The same glass from which the remarkable slipper he had in his possession was made. The only thing he had to remind him that the woman of his dreams really existed.

"Where . . . ?"

"Abandoned by the side of the road," the Duke replied.

Kit blinked, trying to understand what this meant. "And have you found her?"

"The girl? No. She has disappeared." The Grand Duke spoke as if this were obvious.

"There must be some reason she vanished," the king exclaimed for not the first time. "Perhaps she has been prevented from speaking. . . ."

The Grand Duke coughed. "It pains me to say this, Your Highness, but has it occurred to you that a maiden might not return your feelings?"

Kit felt as though the Duke had punctured him with a sword. It was one thing for Kit to think that way; it was another to hear his fears spoken back to him.

The Captain stepped forward, protective of his friend.

But the Duke was not finished. "She may see you as our enemies do: the callow, naive princeling of a weak little monarchy? Perhaps she simply does not love you."

"Grand Duke!" the Captain exclaimed.

Kit met the Duke's gaze, lowering his voice. "I

knew you were cynical, Grand Duke. I did not know you were cruel."

The Grand Duke stepped back and bowed. "The world is cruel, Your Highness, not I."

The king felt a hand on his shoulder. "Don't lose heart, Kit," the Captain said.

"On the contrary. Lose heart and gain wisdom," the Grand Duke said, correcting the man. "The people need to know that the kingdom is secure. That the king has a queen, and the land may have an heir. They want to face the future with certainty."

Kit stepped toward the Duke. "Agreed. Then let us be certain." He gestured at the throne behind him. His father's last words about the Duke echoed in his head.

The Grand Duke will never rule so long as you are not mastered by him.

"Now I am king," Kit continued sternly. "And I say we must seek out the mystery princess. Even if she does not want to be found. I have to see her again." He locked eyes with the Duke once more, seeing the look of surprise on the man's face. "It is my command."

The Grand Duke replaced his stunned expression with a more neutral one. "As you will, Your Majesty. But if she is not found, then for the good of the king-dom, you *must* marry the princess Chelina."

Kit thought that over. He realized the Duke would

not cooperate, would not search for the mystery girl with at least minimal effort, if he did not think Kit would acquiesce to these terms, "for the good of the kingdom."

"Very well. It's agreed," he said. "But you will spare no effort."

"I give you my word," the Grand Duke said, bowing.

As the Duke exited the throne room, Kit exchanged looks with the Captain, both in silent agreement that the Duke's "word" was not one worth having.

Chapter 21

HE grand search for the mystery princess was to commence the following morning. Knowing that the Duke would not exactly devote all his energy to the cause, Kit and the Captain devised a plan in the candlelight of Kit's chambers.

"They should be the right size," the Captain said, handing Kit a soldier's uniform and hooded coat.

"Excellent," Kit said. He held the ensemble against his person and looked into the ornate mirror across from him. "This will do just fine."

Placing the rest of the outfit on a chair, he slid the coat on and lowered the hood over his face. "Do you know me?"

The Captain peered at him, scrutinizing the disguise. "Not in the least, Your Highness," he assured his friend. "But will you be able to see at all?"

"Well enough. Besides, I know the trusty Captain of the Guard will warn me if I am about to run into a ditch or fall off my horse or something."

The Captain snorted. "Yes, but that might prove difficult to explain to the Grand Duke."

Kit laughed. He knew his orders to try the slipper on each and every maiden of the land would be carried out if he was there to make sure they were. And with his anonymity, he would be able to observe both the Duke and the maidens. He would immediately know the impostors, and perhaps he would be able to spot *her* in a crowd.

The king was so caught up in his thoughts that he did not realize the Captain was studying him thoughtfully, a worried expression on his face. "You truly love this maiden, don't you, My Liege?"

"I do," Kit said. "I know I've only spent time with her those two occasions. But she is like no one else I've ever met." Kit paused, searching for the words to explain the impression she had made on him. "She at once says all the things I've thought about but have been hesitant to say aloud my entire life and challenges me to think more deeply about the world."

"Good qualities in a queen," the Captain observed.

"Yes, if . . ." Kit stopped, letting all the "ifs" float in the air. *If* they found her. *If* she felt the same way about him. *If* she wasn't already betrothed to someone else by now.

The Captain walked over to his friend, patting his shoulder. "Do not worry, Kit. The Duke said all of those things so that you would marry Princess Chelina. It was quite evident by the way that woman looked at you at the ball that she was smitten with you, as well. We will find her."

Kit smiled gratefully. If the Captain was right, he'd be face-to-face with the love of his life by the end of the soldiers' search. The next morning could not come soon enough.

The delegation of soldiers rode through the main town first, led by the Grand Duke and the Captain of the Guard. The Captain knocked on the doors of residences and shops alike, asking to see each and every maiden within.

They were met with a variety of reactions to this request. Some shrieked with delight. Others stoically invited the entire troop inside, as though they were displaying their loyalty to their king by presenting every eligible foot they could offer. One commonality all of the homes shared was the palpable air of excitement. More than once, Kit wondered if this was all rather silly. But the slipper was all he had to go on to find *her*.

For Kit could not shake the feeling that something bad had happened to the mystery woman. Something to prevent her from meeting with him. If he found her and she said she did not want to marry him, he could live with that. He just had to make sure that she was all right.

From his place in the back of the troop, Kit quietly observed the Grand Duke. For every maiden who came forward, the man would order the Captain to present the sparkling glass slipper, which rested on a velvet cushion inside a wooden box.

The look of disdain was plain on the Grand Duke's face. It was ever more obvious when the woman trying on the glass shoe was not of aristocratic rank. Kit had always known the Grand Duke to be a bit of a snob, but he'd never thought the man would be outright rude to those he deemed inferior. A discussion would certainly be had with him about that when the search was concluded.

Unfortunately, that would probably be a while still. They had tried the slipper on all sorts of feet—on a middle-aged chef's foot that had been so smelly the soldiers had had to cover their noses with kerchiefs; on the foot of a woman so determined to make the slipper fit that she toppled out of her chair and asked, "Can I try the other foot?"; and even on the foot of a woman old enough to be Kit's grandmother.

From the town square, the troops headed to the country. They were invited into the large, opulent parlors of the wealthier citizens, as well as the simple and clean hearths of the poor. In the courtyard of a country inn, an entire line of women tried their luck to no avail.

The Grand Duke's weariness became more than apparent when he suddenly announced that they were finished. "Enough folly. Not a foot will suit this accursed shoe," he cried as they galloped along a country road. "Back to the palace, Captain."

"We're not done yet, Your Grace," the Captain replied, pointing to a stone estate, hazy in the distance.

Well spotted, Captain, Kit thought, silently cheering his friend's steadfastness, as well as his good vision.

The Duke turned to look. "We've been there already."

The Captain shook his head. "We have not, Your Grace."

The Duke seemed quite annoyed now. "Very well," he conceded. "We can tell His Highness that we have searched *every* house in the kingdom." He harrumphed, leading his horse and the rest of the troop toward the estate.

You most certainly can, Kit thought, pulling his hood closer around his head.

Moments later, the Grand Duke and the Captain were at the door of the last house while the rest of the men dismounted.

A woman holding a fluffy gray cat answered the door. She looked at the Grand Duke. Surprise and recognition flickered on her face at the sight of him.

"A moment of your time, good lady," the Grand Duke said.

"Of course, Your Grace," the woman said, recovering her composure. She curtsied and then opened the door wider so that they might enter.

Escorting them to the parlor, the woman presented two young girls in dresses of blinding yellow and foamy pink.

"These are your daughters?" the Grand Duke asked.

"Yes, Your Grace," the woman said, elbowing one of them in a not-so-subtle manner to make the girl stand straighter.

The Duke repeated the sentence he'd been uttering all day: "They are the only maidens in the house?" However, there was an odd tone of amusement in his voice now, a stark change from the bored tenor he'd been using before.

"Yes," the mother replied, pushing her daughters toward a worn love seat. The two girls flopped down on it, taking their boots off and jetting their stocking-clad feet forward.

The Grand Duke nodded at the Captain, who brought the ornamental wooden box containing the cushion and the stunning glass slipper to the girls. The Captain knelt before them, holding the slipper out as he had done a hundred times that day.

The one wearing yellow shoved her foot into the slipper. And though her foot was quite obviously far too wide for the sparkling shoe, she pushed down on the Captain's head, contorting her foot this way and that as though that would make it fit.

"How strange," the girl said, grimacing. "It fit so well at the ball."

Kit saw her mother roll her eyes.

"Enough!" the Grand Duke barked. "Young miss, you will please leave off this spectacle."

Her sister scoffed. "I could have *told* you it wasn't her." Then, shaking her own foot at the Captain, she waited for him to place the slipper on it.

Unlike it had for the girl's sister, the top of the shoe fit her toes. But the rest of her foot was far too long, her heel hanging off the back of it. The girl sighed,

clearly seeing the futility in trying to wedge it in any farther.

Kit almost laughed out loud. These girls had obviously wanted the slipper to fit for less than noble reasons. He'd seen many of that type on the search—preening girls who wanted nothing to do with him, but merely wanted access to his throne. Then his heart sank as he realized this was the last house in the kingdom.

And they had not found her.

The Grand Duke clapped his hands, clearly satisfied with this conclusion. "Very well," he said. "Since there is no other maiden, our task is done. The prince will be disappointed."

The use of the word *prince* instead of *king* was not lost on Kit. He had known that the Grand Duke had never agreed with his views. Now it was clear the Grand Duke did not respect him as a ruler at all. It was just another blow on an already very upsetting day.

"Ah, well," the mother said, shrugging. "It is the way of the world. But fate may yet be kind to us, girls." Kit thought he saw her wink at the Grand Duke, momentarily breaking him out of his depression.

What in blazes is going on here?

The Grand Duke kissed the woman's hand. "Indeed, madam. You are as wise as you are beautiful." Then he snapped his fingers. The troop headed out of the parlor and through the front door. They were just about to mount their horses when the distinct sounds of a woman singing floated toward them.

> *"Let the birds sing, dilly dilly,*
> *and the lambs play.*
> *We shall be safe, dilly dilly,*
> *out of harm's way."*

Kit stopped, frozen to his spot as his heart leaped out of his chest. That voice.

"Do you hear that, Your Grace?" the Captain asked the Grand Duke.

The Duke brushed him off, turning to his horse. "Let's be off, Captain."

But the Captain did not waver. He held a hand in the air. "Just a moment . . ." Then, turning to the scowling woman standing at the doorway, he asked, "Madam, there is no other maiden in your house?"

"None," the woman answered quickly.

"Then has your cat learned to sing?" the Captain countered.

Kit suppressed laughter. Oh, he was glorious, that Captain!

Just then, the singing resumed, rendering everyone silent.

> *"Lavender's green, dilly dilly.*
> *Lavender's blue.*
> *You must love me*
> *for I love you."*

The other men in the troop cocked their heads and squinted, wondering from where such sweet singing was coming.

"We've had enough playacting, Captain," the Duke said, bristling. "Let's be *off.*" He repeated the order more emphatically.

The Captain stared at him. "But she's lying, Your Grace," he said, gesturing back to the woman at the door.

Kit quietly walked around the other soldiers and horses, sidling up to the Duke.

The Grand Duke seized the slipper's wooden box from the Captain. "Nonsense!" he cried. "I trust the lady. We're leaving!" He thrust the box into the hands of the nearest soldier . . .

. . . who happened to be Kit.

Kit smiled. *I suppose now is as good a time as any.* "Thank you," he said, pulling back his hood.

The Grand Duke turned a shade of crimson, sputtering in shock. "You—Your Highness!"

The woman at the door, equally flushed, dropped into a low curtsy. Her daughters flooded behind her to get a better look. "Your Highness!" they cried.

And yet the singing continued as though the singer was oblivious to the turn of events.

"Lavender's green, dilly dilly . . ."

Kit tilted his head at the sound. "What sweet singing," he observed. "It makes me want to tarry just a little." Then, grinning at the Captain, he asked, "Captain, will you be so good as to investigate?"

The Captain bowed low toward the king, sharing a conspiratorial smile with his friend. "It would be my pleasure, Your Highness."

The Captain moved to enter the house again. "Come along, then, madam," he told the woman as he brushed past her.

The Grand Duke stepped toward Kit, attempting to explain. "Your Highness—"

"Not now," Kit said, following the Captain back inside. "There are more important matters at hand. There will be more than enough time later for your sniveling."

Kit reveled in the look of outrage and shock on the Grand Duke's face before heading into the home's parlor. He sat down on the love seat where the girls had tried on the slipper.

Then he composed himself, taking a deep breath. This could very well be it: the moment he'd been waiting for all his life.

CINDERELLA

Chapter 22

SITTING atop her makeshift bed, Cinderella closed her eyes, stretching her neck from side to side. It had been a trying couple of days. After it had become clear that the door would not budge no matter how much weight she pushed against it, she had run through the gamut of emotions, from bitter anger at her stepmother to grief at the thought of losing Kit.

"Have courage, be kind," her mother had said. And Cinderella had tried. But in spite of all her courage and kindness, she had lost everything she'd loved.

And then, sitting against the cold wooden door, tears streaming down her face, she'd had an epiphany. She'd done what was best for Kit and the entire kingdom. She'd had the courage to do the hardest thing, to refuse the new life she desperately wanted to save others. This was the person she'd always wanted to be, the person her parents would have been proud of.

And that was enough to let the pain and anger and bitterness go. Her stepmother had thrown all she'd had at her, and it still wasn't enough to break Cinderella. Lady Tremaine could not control her. If she'd learned anything from her stepmother—that cold, unhappy woman—it was that a person was the master of her own fate and of her own happiness.

Therefore, Cinderella decided to choose to be happy. She would look fondly on her memories of her parents, of Kit in the forest, of her time at the ball. Those thoughts would keep her warm throughout the cold of winter and feed her when there was not enough to eat.

At that moment, Cinderella wondered what her parents would do if they were there. Before she even realized it, she started to sing her mother's tune again, inventing new lyrics that she knew her father would appreciate:

"The sheep are grazing, dilly dilly.
The pretty sparrows soar.
'Nothing will come of nothing,' dilly dilly.
So I shall do more."

Suddenly, she felt a small tug at her feet. Her mouse friends were pulling at the bottom of her dress.

Cinderella looked down, gently patting their heads with her index finger.

"Yes," she told them. "A dance sounds like a fine idea." She rose and started to waltz around the room to her song. But this did not seem to please the mice. In fact, Jacqueline and Gus scurried to the window while Esau and Jacob kept tugging at Cinderella's dress.

Laughing at their silly antics, Cinderella strode to the window. The late-afternoon sun glowed upon her. She looked out at the horizon, breathing in the fresh air.

"Let the birds sing, dilly dilly,
and the lambs play.
We shall be safe, dilly dilly,
out of harm's way."

Her voice was clear and strong, which was just how Cinderella felt. In that moment, singing the tune of her mother's lullaby, creating her own lyrics, Cinderella was perfectly at peace.

Suddenly, the attic door swung open, interrupting Cinderella's song. Cinderella stared as her stepmother and a tall man in uniform walked inside.

"There!" Lady Tremaine spat out the words, clearly agitated. "No one of importance."

"We'll see about that," the man said. Then, as he looked at Cinderella, his gaze softened. He nodded at her. "Miss."

To say that her sudden visitors surprised Cinderella would be an understatement. But she curtsied at the soldier, trying to regain her composure. This was Kit's friend, she realized. The Captain of the Guard!

"You are requested and required to present yourself to your king." The Captain's words were grand, but his tone was gentle.

Cinderella opened her mouth to reply, though what she would say, she did not know.

Suddenly, Lady Tremaine spoke instead, advancing toward her. "I forbid you to do this!"

"And I forbid you to forbid her," the Captain told the woman. "Who are you to stop an officer of the king? Are you an empress? A saint? A deity?"

Lady Tremaine stood taller. "I am her *mother*."

Something inside Cinderella snapped. "You have never been, and you never will be, my mother," she said, her voice low and steady.

"Come now, miss," the Captain said to Cinderella, gesturing toward the open door.

Cinderella began to follow him when she heard

Lady Tremaine whisper fiercely behind her, "Remember who you are, you wretch!"

Pausing in her tracks without turning around, Cinderella smiled. Of course, Lady Tremaine had meant this to dampen her spirit. But Cinderella did remember who she was, and this gave her the courage to follow the Captain out of the attic and down the staircase.

Before walking inside the parlor, Cinderella took a deep breath. This was it. The time to be honest. Nodding at the Captain of the Guard, she glided through the door. Her heart started to thump when she saw Kit jump up from the couch on which he'd been sitting. He was holding her lost glass slipper.

The young king walked over to her, searching her eyes. "Who are you?" He did not ask it accusingly or even confusedly. He genuinely wanted to know.

"I am Cinderella," she replied.

Anastasia and Drisella tittered from the other side of the room. Kit whirled around to them, rendering them silent with his disapproving look.

"Your Highness," Cinderella began. "I am no

princess. I have no carriage. I have no gown. No parents, and no dowry." She glanced down at the sparkling shoe in his hands. "I do not even know if that beautiful slipper will fit."

She paused, collecting her thoughts. "But if it does, will you take me as I am? An honest country girl who loves you?"

Kit's face broke into a broad smile at the words. He seemed to be relieved by her declaration. "I will."

He knelt in front of her, holding the slipper up. "Please," he said softly. Cinderella sat herself down on the couch. It was just like the moment at the swing. Gingerly, Cinderella slid her foot into the shoe. It was a perfect fit.

She met Kit's eyes, and they looked at each other, lost in the moment. Then, taking the sparkling shoe off and replacing it with her worn slipper, Cinderella rose and took Kit's arm in hers.

"Cinderella!" Drisella cried.

"*Ella!*" Anastasia corrected her sister.

Cinderella looked up to see that her stepsisters were hastily smiling at her. They were even curtsying. The Grand Duke, his face ashen, hovered nearby. He bowed before them.

"My dear sister!" Drisella said, walking toward Cinderella. "I'm sorry—"

"So very sorry!" Anastasia interjected.

Cinderella did not respond. She merely smiled at them, walking with Kit toward the front door.

Lady Tremaine was standing on the staircase, in the very spot where she'd torn Cinderella's mother's dress. She glowered at Cinderella and Kit, seemingly at a loss for words.

Just as she and Kit were about to walk through the front door and head to their new life together, Cinderella paused. She couldn't leave it like that.

Turning around, she told her stepmother the kindest words she knew: "I forgive you."

And with that, the good, honest country girl and the dreamy, thoughtful king were on their way.

Epilogue

IT was a snowy winter day, one that might have been fit for reading by a warm fire, or taking tea, had it been an ordinary day. But for this small kingdom, the day was extraordinary.

"We must have a portrait of you painted," Kit told Cinderella as they walked the hall of the royal gallery. Hanging next to Kit's portrait were the portraits of King Frederick and Cinderella's parents.

"Oh, no," she replied, a twinkle in her eye. "I *do* hate myself in paintings."

They shared a smile, remembering when he'd said those words on that eventful night many months earlier.

Kit formed his face into a playful pout. "Be kind."

"And have courage," Cinderella added, taking his arm.

"And all will be well," the king finished.

They stopped in front of the set of doors that led to the palace terrace.

"Are you ready?" Cinderella asked.

Kit smiled, leaning in to rest his forehead on hers. "For anything, so long as it's with you."

Looking up at Kit, Cinderella returned his smile.

Then, together, the two flung the doors open and stepped onto the terrace. The snow-covered plaza below was filled with people, well-wishers from far and wide, waiting to catch a glimpse of the king and his new queen.

They gasped and cheered at the sight of the royal couple waving at them—her in her ivory chiffon wedding gown decorated with embroidered flowers, and him in his blue-and-gold tunic. They were the picture of elegance and love.

"My queen," Kit said, turning toward her.

Cinderella smiled. "My Kit."

The two leaned in and shared a sweet kiss, much to the delight of the crowd below. They knew that the king, and his new queen, the good, honest country girl, would rule peaceably and justly.

There was no question where Kit and Cinderella would spend their honeymoon. As their simple carriage pulled around the bend, Cinderella felt a surge of excitement. Kit's one experience at the estate had been a bit distracted. She couldn't wait to share with him the place that held so many memories for her.

As Galahad slowed to a stop, Cinderella and Kit squeezed each other's hands before letting go. Cinderella looked down to admire her mother's ruby ring twinkling up at her before she followed Kit out of the carriage. There, in front of the fountain, stood the former captain of the guard, waiting to greet them.

Kit's friend had overseen the Tremaines' move to a new home and the restoration of the estate to its former glory. The old staff, shepherds, and farmers who'd wanted to return were rehired. For this would be a full-fledged working household again, as well as a place where Kit and Cinderella could get away.

"Much as I appreciate the new dukedom, My Liege, I wonder if I might ask you to do one more thing for me," the new grand duke said.

"Anything, Your Grace," Kit replied.

His friend's face broke into a grin. "Live happily ever after."

Cinderella smiled as she and the king responded in unison. "We will."

With that, the Grand Duke and his men mounted their horses and cantered back to the palace. And Cinderella led Kit inside.

She looked around, seeing her father's books back on their shelves, her mother's portrait displayed in the parlor. She sighed contently. Then, turning to her new husband, she said, "Welcome to my home."

THE END